Butcher Road

MW01087438

Jon Athan

For more information on this book or the
author, please visit www.jon-athan.com. General
inquiries are welcome.

Facebook:
https://www.facebook.com/AuthorJonAthan
Twitter: @Jonny_Athan
Contact: info@jon-athan.com

Cover designed by **Sean Lowery**:
http://highimpactcovers.com/

ISBN-10: 978-1543032574
ISBN-13: 1543032575

Thank you for the support!

WARNING

This book contains scenes of intense violence and unpleasant themes. Some parts of this book may be considered violent, cruel, disturbing, or unusual. Certain implications may also trigger strong emotional responses. This book is *not* intended for those easily offended or appalled. Please enjoy at your own discretion.

Table of Contents

Chapter One...1
Chapter Two...9
Chapter Three...21
Chapter Four..29
Chapter Five..37
Chapter Six...49
Chapter Seven...57
Chapter Eight...69
Chapter Nine..77
Chapter Ten...89
Chapter Eleven..99
Chapter Twelve...113
Chapter Thirteen...125
Chapter Fourteen...141
Chapter Fifteen..157

Chapter One

A Long Drive

"This is Delores Evans with the top news story of the hour. Reports indicate a local graveyard was vandalized and defiled late last night. Like a scene from a horror movie, several graves were desecrated and several bodies were exhumed. Many of the unearthed corpses were left on the premises, abused and ravaged. Deputies also believe some of the recently buried bodies may have been stolen. We are not certain if this has anything to do with the rampant human trafficking problem facing our state, but we will continue to press the Sheriff for more details. As of now, the area has been cordoned off by emergency personnel. Should you be concerned about the status of a loved one buried at the Bright–"

The grotesque radio broadcast was disrupted by the sound of grating static. The obnoxious racket blared through the speakers, wafting through the interior of the sedan. With the turn of a knob, the white noise ended. Only the sound of the purring engine and whizzing wind dominated the spacious sedan. The simple sounds were tranquil.

From the passenger seat, Anna Cole asked, "Do you have a CD we can listen to?" She leaned forward and opened the glove department. As she browsed through the sheets of paper and tangled cords, Anna asked, "Do you have one of those... those auxiliary cables so I can at least plug in my phone? I thought you had one in here..."

Austin Barnes gripped the steering wheel and kept his eyes locked on the narrow road ahead. He watched as the scorching pavement scrolled beneath the black sedan with each passing mile. The view was inexplicably hypnotizing – endless pavement. He preferred silence to sensationalized news and pop music garbage, but he knew Anna would not allow it. She was a persistent young woman with a questionable taste for music.

Austin said, "Nope. I don't have a CD or a cable. Hardly anyone even listens to CDs these days anyway. You might as well be asking me for a cassette tape. I probably have a cable in the trunk or in my bag, but I don't have one up here." He glanced at Anna and said, "You're out of luck."

Austin smirked as he gazed into his girlfriend's glowing blue eyes – diamonds atop mountains of shimmering snow. Anna stood with a petite shape, five-three with a delicate figure. She had her beach blonde hair tied in a tousled bun, strands dangling every which way. She wore a white tank top, blue jeans, and black boots. She could be childish at times, certainly puckish during others, but Austin adored every bit of her.

Austin turned towards the straight road and said, "I'll take it out of the trunk the next time we stop. You can listen to your shit music then."

Anna chuckled and shook her head. She rolled her eyes and said, "Thanks, *sweetie.* Now, we wouldn't happen to be stopping any time soon, would we?"

"Are you kidding me? We're not going to waste time right now. I'll get it when we stop next time. *I promise.*"

"Okay, okay. I'm just saying, it might be a boring trip without some music. That's all, that's all..."

Anna childishly giggled as she rolled her eyes towards her boyfriend. She couldn't contain her joy, she could not suppress her laughter. She loved goading the man – it was part of her flirtatious demeanor. Anna injected a sense of energy and passion into the relationship, keeping the heartbeat thrumming. She gently drummed her fingertips on Austin's forearm, watching him with kittenish eyes. *Seduction could work,* she thought, *or maybe some irritation.*

Austin was tall and strong – lean, muscular, sinewy. He had long dark brown hair with some stubble on his chiseled jawline. His brown eyes were blocked by his voguish sunglasses. He wore a blue-and-white plaid button-up shirt with the sleeves rolled up on top of a white t-shirt. His blue jeans and brown boots were fairly standard. He was arguably handsome, but he was not obsessed with his appearance. His ego was dormant most of the time.

Anna sighed as she leaned back in her seat. As the air conditioning caressed her moist brow, she asked, "You think we'll find a gas station any time soon? I *really* want that cable..."

Austin shook his head and said, "I don't know, Anna. I told you to pack everything you needed, remember?"

"Come on, you gave me less than an hour to get ready..."

"That's because you weren't supposed to be joining me anyway, remember? I didn't invite you. I told you it was only a business trip and I'd be back in two, maybe three days. *Of course,* you wanted to tag along like always. Remember, though, I never invited you. Don't blame me for anything, okay? It's all on you this time."

Anna crossed her arms, huffing and puffing like a child preparing to throw a tantrum. Yet, she could not keep the facade afloat. She wasn't a trained actress, she had not mastered the steady 'poker face.' She held her hand to her mouth as she burst into a playful guffaw. Austin chuckled and shook his head – *my girl.*

Anna said, "I know, I know. I just didn't want you to make this drive alone. I wasn't going to let you drive 500 miles by yourself. You know how I get. It worries me. It's the anxiety. This sort of trip is... *dangerous.*"

Austin smiled smugly and said, "Well, I really don't see what your presence is going to do, sweetheart. You can't fight, you're not very athletic, and you can't even change a tire. It's probably more dangerous with you around."

"Yeah, but I can use a phone and I can call for help. And, when you're too damn stubborn to ask for directions, you can let me do it. So, yeah, I can be helpful when you need it. I'm much more helpful than one of those bimbos in a horror movie, that's for sure."

Austin shook his head and smirked, scoffing at Anna's definition of help. Anna simply turned in her seat and gazed out the window. The pair cruised in silence, soaking in the tranquility. There was a mountainous region to the right, barely visible from afar. To the left, the land was flat and dry. The desolate road was surrounded by dry shrubs and swathes of desert. The bushes rustled with the wind and the dirt majestically danced with each gust. The couple only spotted an oncoming driver every few minutes. The route was lonely, practically abandoned by humanity.

Anna shuffled in her seat, looking for the most comfortable position possible. She was fidgety and restless, bothered by the sheer boredom. She sought a form of entertainment, any variety of amusement to sweep her away. She glanced at the digital clock on the radio – *4:35 PM.* Time seemed to move slower during the most monotonous trips. Anna sighed loudly, blatantly trying to grab Austin's attention.

She said, "I'm sorry. This is just too boring, Austin. Why couldn't you just buy a plane ticket? Hmm? Why couldn't we do this the easy way? I mean, a five-hour road trip? *Really?* Who drives for that long nowadays?"

Austin rebutted, "And, where do you think I would get the money for a plane ticket? Were you going to pay for it?" Anna did not respond, biting her tongue and looking away. Austin nodded and said, "Yeah, I thought so."

Anna sighed again – each sigh grew louder with

the swelling boredom. She kicked her feet up on the dashboard and leaned back in her seat, shielding herself from the blistering sun with the car's shadows. With her nonchalant pose, she painted a portrait of tedium. She was not trying to be disrespectful, she simply could not stand the boredom. Her mind wandered between thoughts: *What can we talk about? What games can we play?* There weren't many options on the table. *Oh, look at that cactus. Maybe we can get water from it.*

As she stared at the passing rocks and cacti, Anna asked, "So, do you know any shortcuts?"

Austin responded, "What kind of shortcuts do you expect to find out here? It's a straight road, leading directly to our destination. Nothing more, nothing less. There's not going to be some sort of magical route that will make this go by any faster."

"Yeah, you're right. Don't bother taking any scenic routes, either. It's just going to be a waste of time. I mean, what are we going to look at? Rocks and dirt?"

Austin nodded and said, "I wouldn't have even considered it. Shortcuts, scenic routes... You're just asking for trouble. I'm not going through some back-road to get eaten by some inbred cannibals in the hills. No, I'm not taking those chances."

Anna huffed, then she said, "I think you're taking horror movies a bit too seriously."

"No, no. Horror movies, books, *fiction...* It's all derived from human nature. It's inspired by real events. If it's not, it's at least created by a real person. You understand what I'm saying? Someone sits there and thinks about all of the most terrifying situations that could possibly happen. It's... It's all based on reality. I think the problem is: we *don't* take horror films seriously enough. Maybe then, kids would stop dying at camps."

Anna giggled, then she glanced at Austin. She said, "But, that only happens in movies. When was the last time you heard about some kids getting slaughtered at a camp?"

Austin opened his mouth to speak, but the words would not flow through his lips. His vocabulary was wiped with Anna's counter. He contemplated, browsing through months of grisly news, but he couldn't find anything of use. He could only grin and nod. His speech sounded perfectly rational and intelligent in his mind.

Austin said, "Maybe it doesn't happen at camps anymore, but that's because we *learned* from those movies. We stopped underestimating kids that drowned in lakes. Besides, I'm sure there have been some murders in some cabins recently. Hell, I'm sure someone's getting killed in a cabin right now. I'm willing to bet on it."

"Okay, so what are you betting?"

Austin glanced at Anna, then he said, "Never mind."

Anna and Austin shared a genuine chuckle, laughing with sincere joy. Anna gently slapped Austin's lean forearm and said, "You can be a real idiot sometimes, Austin, but I love you for it..."

Chapter Two

An Accident

The luxurious sedan cruised down the narrow road, racing against the falling sun. The blinding sun doused the desert area with a scorching heat. The hot spell was mesmerizing, enough to make a sane man hallucinate. The interior of the vehicle, fortunately, benefited from the air conditioning. The cold breeze could not trump the power of the sun, but it offered some comfort.

As a cherry-red pickup truck hurtled down the oncoming lane, Austin whispered, "First car in thirty minutes... Where are you off to in such a hurry?"

Staring at the ceiling of the car, Anna said, "We should be driving faster, too. I want to get into a hotel with *real* air conditioning, hop into the pool, sip a martini, relax..." She grunted and groaned as she turned towards Austin. Pouting with glimmering eyes, Anna said, "You'll hate me for asking this, but... Are we there yet?"

Austin yawned, then he said, "Nope. And, I hate you for asking."

Anna frowned and said, "I know."

"It's such a stupid question. I mean, you can see we're not there yet, so what's the point of asking? It doesn't make sense."

"Yeah, it makes about as much sense as being afraid of 'cannibals in the hills.' But, hey, I'm not the type to judge."

Austin chuckled, then he said, "Yeah, yeah, I get it..."

Austin and Anna were flung forward in their seats as the car skidded to an abrupt stop. The sound of screeching wheels echoed through the desolate environment, howling like wolves to the moon. The startled pair were solely kept seated by the tight seat belts. The couple sat in absolute silence, astonished for different reasons. With his foot firmly planted on the brake pedal, Austin glanced over his shoulder, peering through the back window.

With her palms planted on the dashboard, Anna said, "I almost smashed my head, Austin. I... I could have died right now. Why the hell did you do that?" Austin did not respond. His fearful eyes were locked on the rear window. Anna loudly swallowed, then she asked, "What's wrong with you? What's going on?"

Austin pointed back and said, "There's... There's a wagon back there. Off the road."

"A wagon?"

"Yeah, *a wagon.* A–A station wagon... Off the road on your side. It looks like there was some sort of accident."

Anna rolled her window down. She protruded her head from the opening and stared at the side of the road. Like Austin explained, there was a clove-brown station wagon off the side of the road a few dozen meters back. The vehicle appeared to have rolled to a stop at the bottom of a ditch. Billowing white fumes spewed from the engine, but there was no sign of a fire.

Anna returned to her seat and said, "Okay, so... there was an accident. Why the hell did you stop so suddenly? You could have ended up like them. We could have seriously hurt our necks. You know, *whiplash,* right? Shit..." Anna sniffled as she wiped the sweat from her glistening forehead. She shook her head and said, "They were probably taken to a hospital. Someone will probably come out for the car later. No big deal."

Without taking his eyes off the vehicle, Austin explained, "I... I think I saw someone in that wagon, Anna. There was... I could have swore I caught a glimpse of some blood on their windows, too. It was red. The whole interior of that car was *red.* I swear, I saw it."

Anna stared at her boyfriend, trying her best to decipher his intentions. Yet, she found herself baffled by Austin's behavior. She was the devious rascal, always trying to inject some fun into the relationship. Austin's humor did not often meander into morbid territory. From the horrified look in his eyes, she could see he was bewildered.

Anna asked, "Are you serious?"

Austin turned towards his girlfriend. He gazed into her glimmering eyes and said, "There was blood everywhere. I know what I saw."

Anna ran her fingers through her hair, perturbed by Austin's honesty. She protruded her head from the opening and glanced back at the wagon. She could see the wrecked vehicle, but she could not see the blood. Yet, she refused to take a chance. She grabbed her cell phone from the dashboard, then she swiped her finger across the touchscreen.

Austin asked, "You're calling the police?"

Anna said, "I don't have any reception out here, but we should still have emergency services. I can still call the police, right?"

Austin did not have a definitive answer to share. Anna tapped the screen, then she held the phone to her ear. To her utter dismay, the call did not connect. The couple had stumbled into a dead zone, incapable of receiving radio messages or calling for help.

As Anna softly whimpered, Austin leaned forward and said, "Listen, I'm going to go out there and see if I can help."

Teary-eyed, Anna asked, "Are you kidding me, Austin? Are you serious?"

"I'm serious. Like you said, this isn't a horror movie and those people may need help. Every second matters in a situation like this. I'll go down there as fast as possible. If I see any signs of danger or anything like that, I'll come running back and we'll drive out of here. Okay? I want you to walk around right here and try to find some service. That sound good to you?"

Anna wiped the tears from her blushed cheeks and nodded. As she despondently stared at her lap, she said, "Okay..."

***

Austin slowly exited the vehicle. He stood on his tiptoes and stared down the narrow road. He could see the heat waves dancing above the sweltering pavement. He had hoped the discovery was nothing but a mirage. To his disappointment, there were no other cars in sight. The cavalry was not arriving with emergency aid – reinforcements were nonexistent.

Anna exited the vehicle, carefully closing the door behind her – like if the car would crumble with too much force. She glanced at her boyfriend with nervous eyes, then she walked towards the side of the road. She watched each step, ensuring she didn't tumble down the hill. The feisty young woman held her cellphone up and hoped for a bar of reception.

Austin whispered, "Okay, I'm coming..."

The young man sauntered down the side of the road, approaching the wagon with caution. With each calculated step, he found himself with a better view of the accident. He bit his bottom lip and shook his head as he caught a glimpse of the blood. The door windows were either cracked or shattered, but the blood remained consistent across the glass. The windshield was also smeared with blood, but it seemed intact. No one was ejected from the vehicle.

A person was slumped back in the driver's seat and another person was slumped forward in the passenger seat. The bloodied people did not move – not a squirm or twitch. From afar, the pair were unidentifiable. With some simple logical contemplation, Austin figured there was a man and a woman in the wagon – much like himself and Anna. He was not interested in pondering the more sinister possibilities.

As he approached, Austin held his shirt to his nose and muttered, "What happened to you? How...

How the..."

Austin was rendered speechless, awed by his discovery. Indeed, a man sat in the driver's seat and a woman rested in the neighboring seat. The couple were brutally slaughtered, drenched in blood like if they had emerged from a crimson pool.

The lanky man was slumped back in his seat. His throat was savagely slit from ear-to-ear. The bloody gash grew thicker due to the weight of the man's head – skin ripping millimeter-by-millimeter. His white button-up shirt and blue jeans were soaked in blood. Through the red garments, Austin could see more puncture wounds. The man was sliced and stabbed. Austin couldn't tell which came first.

The woman's white dress and brunette hair were also stained with blood. Although he could not see her throat, Austin could see she was stabbed across her torso. He safely assumed her throat was slit beneath her hair. Blood dripped from her upper-body – throat, face, head, it did not matter. She was brutalized by a sharp blade.

Judging from the droplets of blood oozing from both victims, their deaths were relatively recent. The seemingly simple accident metamorphosed into a grisly crime scene without warning. The violent scene could not be mistaken for a car crash – the theory was outlandish. The couple were massacred like animals at a slaughterhouse.

Austin leaned towards the vehicle and examined the roadside carnage. He whispered, "Jesus... Someone killed you. I... I don't know what to say to you. I don't know what to do. I've never... I've never seen anything like this before."

Austin inhaled deeply, flustered by his inability to act. He glanced at the back seat and furrowed his brow. The leather seats in the back were smeared with more blood. He could see a bloody handprint on the cushion. A person was missing from the scene – possibly two. The young man was not positive, but the possibility pricked at his mind. He glanced around the wagon, but to no avail. There were no other bodies in sight.

Austin whispered, "Where are you? Where did you go? What happened to you?" He staggered in reverse, getting a better picture of the slaughter. Eyes brimming with tears, Austin repeated, "What happened to you?"

From over Austin's shoulder, Anna loudly gasped – her breath was vacuumed from her tender lungs. She gazed at the crashed wagon with wide, protuberant eyes. Her eyes practically bulged from her skull. She held one hand to her chest and the other to her mouth. Her expression was blatant – she was horrified.

Austin turned towards Anna, then he held her in his arms. As his girlfriend sobbed into his chest, panting and sniffling, Austin gently caressed Anna's hair. Although he was able to adjust to the gory murder, he understood the toll excessive violence took on the everyday psyche. *Some people aren't built like me,* he thought. He offered Anna a sense of security and normality.

Anna asked, "What... What happened to them? Austin, that... that doesn't look like an accident."

Austin nodded and said, "I know, I know. Just don't look at it. Don't think about it."

"How can I *not* think about it? They were... There's so much blood."

Anna turned away from the carnage. She placed her hands on her kneecaps and retched. She couldn't vomit, but the sensation echoed through every limb. She was weakened by the mere sight of blood, enfeebled by the gore. She could handle the most extreme horror movie, but real violence was too much to endure.

Austin gently patted Anna's back and said, "Go up to the road and try to call for help. Try to wave down a car or something, alright? Don't come back down here. I'll come to you. I don't want you to see this."

Wiping the tears from her rosy cheeks, Anna asked, "What are you going to do?"

"I'm just going to check it out a little more. I think there might have been someone else in the car. Someone might be hurt. Go on. Get up there."

***

Anna trudged up the slope, glancing towards the wagon with each wobbling step. She was bothered by the discovery and haunted by the graphic imagery. Yet, like a nosy driver cruising past a violent car accident, she couldn't help but glance back. A neck made of rubber, she felt compelled to take a final glimpse of the wreck.

Anna whispered, "I'm sorry..."

The young woman stumbled towards the center of the road. She stared down the road to her left, then she glanced down the oncoming lane. She could see miles and miles of blistering pavement, but there were no cars in sight. The road was eerily desolate. The massacred couple were left stranded, burning with the torrid heat.

Anna sniffled as she pondered the couple's unfortunate demise. She swiped at her nose, then she retrieved her cellphone. She hopelessly tried to block her sinister thoughts. Merely contemplating the pain left her rattled and disturbed. To her dismay, she was still trapped in a dead zone – the bad news continued to snowball.

As she tightly shut her eyes and stomped, Anna muttered, "Damn it... Damn it..."

Austin examined the interior of the wagon, gliding his eyes across every nook and cranny. Like a dedicated detective, he was searching for evidence – any evidence. He sought a clue, a spark of hope to ignite his unsolicited investigation. Aside from the plentiful blood, there was nothing out of the ordinary.

Austin glanced at the windshield, then up at the ceiling of the vehicle. He licked his lips as he carefully leaned into the car. He avoided eye contact with the slaughtered man, leaning away from the bloodied corpse. He gently pulled on the sun visor. A polaroid photograph slipped out, gliding into his hands.

As he staggered out of the vehicle and examined the photograph, Austin murmured, "Now, where the hell are you?"

The photograph depicted a happy family. The bloodied man inside the wagon stood beside a brunette woman. Austin could put two and two together. A young, dark-haired girl stood between the pair. She resembled the man and woman – *a daughter.* Yet, the presumed daughter was not inside the vehicle. The radio broadcast immediately stampeded through his mind.

Austin whispered, "Human trafficking? *Abduction?*" He glanced around the desert, peering towards the mountainous region. He said, "I hope you weren't in the car, sweetheart. I hope you didn't have to see any of this..."

Bewildered by the innocent image, Austin returned the photograph to the visor. He wiped his hands on his jeans, then he slowly departed the crashed wagon. Like Anna, he couldn't help but look back at the vehicle as he trudged up the slope. Perhaps it was the crimson color, but blood was attractive to the human eye.

Austin asked, "Have you seen anyone?"

Anna shook her head and responded, "No... No, there hasn't been a single car since we stopped." She glanced at the dazzling sun as she sniveled. She said, "The sun will be going down soon. There will be even less cars than now, Austin."

"I know, I know. Were you able to call anyone?"

"No. There was no signal over there, none over here... There's no reception *anywhere* around here. A few meters isn't going to make a difference. We... We have to keep driving. We have to move on and find signal or a gas station or a landline phone. There has to be an emergency phone on the side of the road, right? There has to be something, we just have to keep moving. We can't waste our time standing here doing nothing."

Austin stared at the trunk of the wagon, saddened. He said, "You're right. We're not doing them any good waiting around here. Either the cops will find them or someone else will. We'll report it at our next stop. Come on. Let's get going."

Crestfallen, Anna frowned as she gazed into her boyfriend's eyes. She said, "Thank you..."

Chapter Three

The Hitchhiker

Austin continued driving, unnerved by the disquieting discovery. He was appalled by the violence, sick to his stomach, but he refused to show his overwhelming fear. He wanted to set an example of bravery during a time of terror. He delved into an atrocious pit of horror and trepidation, but he sought to keep his masquerade afloat. The endless road kept his mind off the ruthless realities of life – at least for a moment.

Anna squirmed in the passenger seat, struggling to find comfort. Her skin was crawling, like if cockroaches were scurrying across her body. Brutal murder was not the type of escape she sought from boredom. She tightly clenched her cellphone, checking for signal every other second. There was no reception in the desert environment – one or five miles, it did not make a difference. The attempts were fruitless.

Anna whispered, "Crappy service... Crappy, crappy, *crappy* service... 'Most coverage,' my ass." She glanced back at the rear window, pondering the deaths of the massacred couple. As she turned back in her seat, Anna asked, "What... What do you think did that to them? It couldn't have been an accident, right? I mean, a seat belt can't do that, *right?*"

Austin shook his head and said, "I don't know."

"You saw them. You were with them for a few minutes. You must have some sort of idea."

Austin sternly snapped, "I don't know, okay? *I don't know.*"

Austin tightly gripped the helm and bit his bottom lip. He was agitated by the simple questioning. Anna was not the problem, her voice was not vexing. He could never despise his girlfriend. He simply didn't want to contemplate the heinous possibilities. He grappled with his mind, but the question dominated his thoughts. The idea stabbed at his tender brain for miles. *Who killed them?*

Austin said, "I'm sorry. I just don't know. It was bloody and it was violent. It was *very* violent."

Anna turned her attention to the road and said, "It didn't look like an accident. I guess I should be asking 'who,' right? *Who* could have done that to those people? I mean, I didn't see it like you, but it was all red. It was all blood and..."

Austin interrupted, "You get any signal yet?"

Anna lifted her phone from her lap, gazing at the large screen with vacant eyes. The same mundane symbols could not conjure excitement within her petite body. There was no service for the last mile of the road trip. The circumstances did not seem likely to change within the next mile, either. The pair were driving through barren territory. The couple were better off hoping to catch and train a pigeon to send a message than to use a phone in the middle of nowhere.

Anna responded, "I don't think we'll be making a

call any time soon. Should I try your phone?"

Austin nodded and said, "Sure, it's in my back pocket." As he leaned towards his left and beckoned to Anna, he said, "I don't think it'll make much of a difference since we're on the same damn service, but everything's worth a shot."

As Anna retrieved the sleek black device from her boyfriend's pocket, Austin stepped on the brakes. He slowed the car to a leisurely roll, carefully driving onto the side of the road. Anna glanced at Austin with a furrowed brow. Austin's narrowed eyes were locked on the rear-view mirror.

Anna bit her bottom lip, then she said, "Please, don't tell me it's another accident..."

Austin shook his head and responded, "No, no. Look, it's a hitchhiker. I think he's hurt. He's... He's *bleeding.*"

Anna glanced over her shoulder, peering through the rear window. A man shambled down the road, swinging his right arm and gripping his stomach with his left hand. The man stood a towering six-four, lean and sturdy. He wore a filthy brown checkered button-up shirt. The shirt was stained with blood at the stomach. His blue jeans were also stained with dirt and droplets of blood, and his brown boots were begrimed.

As she gazed at the man with inquisitive eyes, Anna said, "Just keep driving."

Austin said, "Yeah, I will, but... do you think he's seriously injured? Do you think he might have been in that accident?"

"I don't know, but I have a bad feeling about all of

this. Believe me, I'm not a stuck-up bitch. I don't want to leave him behind if he's innocent, but I'm... I don't know, I'm scared of him. He could be anyone, Austin. I think we should keep driving."

Austin nodded and said, "Okay, okay. Let's just get a good look at him, then we'll drive off."

Anna frowned as she stared at the man. The wounded hitchhiker stopped fifteen meters from the sedan. The man had slick black hair with strands dangling every which way. His vibrant blue eyes could be seen from afar, glowing like beacons in a dark abyss. He had a groomed beard covering his well-defined jawline. Despite his injuries, the man was surprisingly suave and debonair. If it weren't for his wounds, he'd be a fairly handsome and charismatic man – a pretty boy.

Anna asked, "Why is he just standing out there? What the hell is he doing?"

Austin whispered, "I have no idea."

Austin and Anna stared at the rear-view mirror, watching the man with narrowed eyes. They examined each minuscule movement, watching every repetitive breath. The couple patiently waited in the comfort of the sedan's air conditioning, but the man did not move forward. The hitchhiker stood in solidarity. He tightly gripped his wounds and his body bounced with each heavy breath, but he did not approach. The reaction was strange, out-of-character for a hitchhiker.

Austin turned towards Anna and said, "Go ask him if he needs a lift."

Wide-eyed, Anna asked, "Are you kidding me?

Look at him. He's standing out there like some sort of creep. You want to invite him into our car?"

"*My car.* He's bleeding, Anna. He's not acting right, sure, but it's probably because he's bleeding out. He's out there in the sun, roasting in the heat for crying out loud. What do you expect? You want him to come prancing over here?"

"I expect you to act a bit more rational at a time like this."

"I am acting rational. You know I'm scared of horror movies. Yeah, yeah, it's funny. But, I'm adding everything together. I saw blood in the back seat of the wagon. That man is bleeding. He's bleeding a lot. And, I mean, there's two of us and only one of him, right? What can he possibly do to us in that condition? Huh? I'm trying to be a good guy here."

Anna rolled her eyes and scoffed, "Good guys always get killed by bad guys. You should know that by now."

Austin ran his fingers through his hair and sniffled as he glanced back at the man. The hitchhiker did not move an inch. The mysterious man coughed and grunted, but he stayed in place like a dog waiting for permission to move. From every logical corner, the man seemed harmless – injured, respectful, and handsome. *What's the worst that can happen?*–Austin thought.

Anna said, "Listen, I understand you want to be a good guy, but what if... what if he was responsible for that car wreck? Huh? What if he's really dangerous? Are you willing to risk both of our lives for some stranger?"

Austin licked his lips, then he said, "Okay. We offer him a lift and, if things don't work out, we ditch him at the nearest gas station. Hell, if I think he's dangerous, I'll kick him out in the middle of nowhere, I promise. Sound good?" Anna hesitated as she glanced back at the man – injured, respectful, handsome, *and dangerous.* Austin said, "You can keep your eyes on him the entire time. Give me a little nudge the moment you feel unsafe and we'll dump him. I mean, the man could die out here if we don't help. He could be innocent and he could *die* because of us."

Anna sighed, then she said, "Fine, fine. You're going to do whatever you want to do anyway. I can't stop you. But, you better bet I'm going to keep my eyes on him, even if you think it's rude. I don't care. I'm not going to take my eyes off that man."

"You can be as rude as you want to be. I just want to help him out and get to the bottom of that crash..."

Austin pushed down on the steering wheel, honking the shrill horn. He glanced back at the man and furrowed his brow. The hitchhiker started walking towards the car, moseying at a snail's pace. The man was oddly polite, waiting for an invite before approaching. His demeanor was not common for a hitchhiker.

Austin whispered, "He's a little strange, I guess..." As the hitchhiker approached, Austin asked, "You okay out here? You need a lift?"

The man smiled and responded, "I'm a little scratched up, yeah, but I'll live. I can sure use a lift, though, if you don't mind me taking you up on that offer."

Austin stared at the man's bloodied shirt, examining the damage. Looking through the holes on his shirt, he could see several wounds on the man's abdomen – puncture wounds and small scratches. A stabbing immediately came to mind, but he wasn't certain. *It must be wounds from the broken glass,* he thought.

Austin said, "We can give you a lift as far as we go. You mind if I ask your name?"

With a charismatic grin plastered on his face, the mysterious man responded, "Dante. Dante Hooper."

Chapter Four

Road Talk

Austin stared down the empty road, watching for any oncoming vehicles. He modestly attempted to cover his anxiety, playing the role of a secure and knowledgeable captain. Anna leaned on the passenger seat door and stared at the rear-view mirror. She watched their guest with a keen eye. Her blatant suspicion was impolite, but she was more concerned with her safety than her mannerisms.

Dante sat towards the center of the back seat. He stared down at his wounds, grimacing with each bump on the road. He did not bother to secure himself with a seat belt. The belt would only aggravate the bloody injury. He appeared lost in his thoughts – lost in the pain. Although he was certainly uncanny, he did not seem malicious. He wasn't a caricature spawned from a horror movie.

Breaking the silence, Dante asked, "So, what are your names? I told you mine, I figured you'd tell me yours. You know, we can get friendly and all."

Austin nodded and said, "Yeah, sure. My name is Austin and this is my girlfriend Anna."

Dante watched Anna through the rear-view mirror. He said, "I don't know if you overheard me when I introduced myself to your boyfriend. My name is Dante. It's nice to meet you, ma'am." Anna did not respond. Dante glanced down at the blood oozing from his stomach and said, "I'm sorry about the blood. I'll try not to get any on your seats. I can be a little messy at times, but this... I don't really know how to deal with this."

Austin said, "Yeah, you know, don't worry about it. I wish I had a first-aid kit in the car, but we're out of luck. I don't really know what to do in this situation, either. I can pull over and get a rag from the trunk if you–"

Dante shook his head and interrupted, "No, no, no. I don't want to stop. We should just keep going. A rag won't do much better than a shirt anyway... I appreciate the offer, though. I really do. Thank you, friend."

Chiming-in, Anna asked, "Do you know how much longer we have to drive until we hit the nearest town or hospital? You know, somewhere safe for all of us?"

Austin glanced at Anna and bit his bottom lip. He was nervous, but he didn't feel any danger. Although he understood her intentions, he feared Anna would aggravate a trivial issue. The words, the timing, and the tone could spiral the pair into madness. The slaughtered couple flashed in his mind, painting his retinas red with blood.

Dante chuckled, coughing and grunting between his clucking. He said, "Yeah, it probably doesn't feel too safe out here, does it? Not under these bloody circumstances, at least... I understand, though. I get it. We should be seeing a gas station soon. I think we can find some supplies there. Well, I hope so..."

Anna inhaled deeply as she stared at Dante. From

the driver's seat, Austin could see she was planning her next move. He could read every crease on her brow and every twinkle in her eyes. His girlfriend was strategizing, maneuvering like a soldier at war. She was surely more capable than a 'bimbo' in a horror movie. Austin bit his tongue and moved aside, allowing her to take the lead.

Anna said, "Listen, Dante, I don't mean to pry, but... Were you involved in that accident back there?" Dante stared directly at Anna – he didn't require the rear-view mirror. Anna turned towards the back seat and said, "I think you understand my suspicions, right? The crashed wagon, the blood... It just looked so horrible and I need to know. I need some... some reassurance or something. What happened back there?"

Dante sighed, then he explained, "Yeah, I was part of that. It was just a really bad accident. If you saw it, then I really don't have to tell you what happened to them... It doesn't seem necessary to me, ma'am. They're dead. They're all dead..."

Visibly worried, Anna glanced at Austin. Austin clenched his jaw and kept his eyes on the road. He was bothered, but he refused to show weakness. Anna was rattled by Dante's demeanor. He seemed simultaneously sincere and devious – a breathing contradiction. Anna couldn't help herself, she felt compelled to delve deeper.

Anna asked, "What happened back there, Dante? It was more than a car accident, wasn't it? There was too much blood, too much violence... I know they're dead, but I don't know *why* they died. What happened?"

Dante gazed at Anna and said, "Well, you're right, miss. You're... You're very perceptive. It was not a normal car accident. It wasn't a bump on the road or a drunk driver. They didn't swerve to dodge a critter or a person on the road. No, it wasn't like that."

"So, what was it?" Austin asked.

Dante nervously chuckled as he wiped the sweat from his brow. He absently stared at the dormant radio and explained, "It all started when we picked up a hitchhiker. A man. *A big man.* Some would probably call him 'eccentric' or 'weird,' but I thought he would be okay. I'm not the type to judge. My father raised me better than that. Unfortunately, this man took advantage of our kindness. We gave him a chance and he attacked us. He..."

Dante sniffled and shook his head, trying to contain his tears. He despondently stared at his lap, clearly ruminating. Austin and Anna watched him with narrowed eyes, examining his sorrowful demeanor. Despite the tears swelling in his eyes, the couple remained suspicious and vigilant. They refused to be duped by the charming hitchhiker.

Dante inhaled deeply, then he said, "Well, he stabbed them. He sliced them. He cut them up real bad. I barely got out alive. I... I heard them screaming, but I couldn't stop running. I told my body to stop, I really did, but I just kept going. Fear gets to you like that sometimes. It controls you. I was lucky you stopped, though. I was running out of energy and that man... That man is probably still out there somewhere..."

Anna gazed into Dante's pensive eyes. He was melancholic, a black cloud poured pessimism onto his head. Yet, she couldn't believe his tale. *A campfire horror story,* she thought, *a hitchhiker's fable.* She was profusely bothered by the disturbing event and their enigmatic guest. Austin sat in silence, minding his business and allowing his girlfriend to pry. He was equally curious.

Anna said, "You didn't mention who you were traveling with. A brother, a sister, a wife, a friend... Who were those people?"

Austin said, "Okay, Anna, maybe we should just leave it. We don't know them and we shouldn't rub salt in fresh wounds. Let's just sit in silence for a while. We should be hitting a gas station soon, right? *Right?*"

Ignoring Austin's question, Dante said, "They were close friends of mine for a while. They helped me get through a rough patch in my life. We were supposed to be enjoying a little road trip, escaping from... from *civilization,* I suppose. I didn't realize it would end up like this, though. It was supposed to be an innocent retreat. We just wanted to leave."

Austin placed more pressure on the gas pedal. Although the hitchhiker sought escape, Austin simply wanted to reach civilization as soon as possible. Anna stared out the passenger seat window, mesmerized by the beautiful sky – tints of blue and orange painted on a soft canvas. Tranquility was welcomed with open arms in the sedan.

Seizing the opportunity to change the subject,

Dante asked, "So, where were you headed?"

Austin responded, "Well, we're headed to Vegas for a photo-shoot. I'm a freelance photographer and I have a gig this week. It's a big step up for my career. Something to add to the portfolio, you know?"

Dante smiled and nodded – *sure.* He glanced at Anna and asked, "So, are you the model or the muse? You look like you could be both if you ask me."

Before Anna could utter a word, Austin explained, "Anna is a tag-along. She's modeled for me before, but she's still in school. She's going to finish up, then we'll see where the world takes us. Hopefully a bright future awaits."

"You're a student? What college do you go to?"

With a pinch of snark in her voice, Anna said, "It's a school. Just a regular school like every other campus in this country. Just a school..."

Dante could take a hint from Anna's dismissive response. He leaned back in his seat and slowly lifted his shirt. There were three puncture wounds spread throughout the left side of his lean stomach. One wound appeared deep and mutilated, the others were precise and clean – *in and out.* His chiseled abs could not protect him against a honed blade.

Anna held her phone up and checked for signal, but to no avail. The dead zone seemed endless. Austin fiddled with the radio, pressing buttons and turning knobs. He glanced at the oncoming lane with each passing second, hoping to encounter a passing car – *any car.* His hope quickly dwindled. The road was desolate.

Austin's eyes widened as he stared at the right side of the road. From afar, he could see a building. With each passing meter, the remote building grew larger. Anna lowered her phone as she caught a glimpse of the small structure. The trio approached a gasoline station. Civilization was a mere mile away.

Chapter Five

The Gasoline Station

The dazzling sun began to set, falling behind the craggy mountains. Slits of balmy sunshine penetrated the hills and doused the desert region for a moment longer. Directly across the entrance of the filling station, the black sedan rolled to a stop next to a green gasoline pump with a white frame. A sign on the building read: *Otto's Auto Gas and Market.* An independent gas station in the middle of nowhere was a rare discovery. The trio escaped a nightmarish experience at an everyday gas station.

Anna gazed at the building with hopeful eyes. Through the pristine windows, she could see the aisles filled with road trip meals, snacks, and magazines. To the left of the double door entrance, a young man in a red polo shirt stood by a cash register. He was phlegmatic, patiently waiting for the end of his shift. Anna couldn't blame him – she did not expect a red carpet for her arrival.

Dante coughed, then he said, "You two go ahead, I'll wait in the car."

Austin furrowed his brow and stared at Dante, astonished. He asked, "You... You want to wait here? *Why?*"

"Well, what do you think? I'm bleeding, man. I shouldn't be walking around and shopping. I'll wait here. Just... Just buy some supplies and I'll patch myself up. Then, we can get going. Hell, if you think you're going to be late, we can even drive while I operate. It won't be a problem for me. I've got good hands."

Dante chuckled as he leaned back in his seat, delirious. Austin and Anna stared at the hitchhiker, then they gazed at each other. The couple were at a lost for words. Dante's shift in demeanor was alarming. His cordial, cooperative personality shifted with their arrival.

Anna shook her head and said, "I think you should come with us. I mean, we're not doctors. We don't know what you need or how you're feeling. I hate to say this, but we're not loaded, either. We offered you a ride, not a dip in our bank accounts."

Dante stared at Anna with a deadpan expression. He huffed, then he asked, "What are you afraid of? You think I'm going to... to steal the car? You think I'm planning something 'underhanded?' What's wrong with you?" He turned towards Austin and asked, "What's wrong with her? Huh? Does she have some trust issues? Or some control issues?"

Austin responded, "There's nothing wrong with her. She's right. You should go in there and pick out your stuff. If you need a buck, I can cover for you, but you need to work with us. We're going to have to use their phone to call 911 anyway. You might as well come in now so we don't have to explain every little detail to the kid. We don't know those details anyway, you understand?"

Dante clenched his jaw, staring at Austin with sharp eyes. He asked, "You're going to call 911?

And... what if I don't want you to call the police? What if I just want to keep going until we hit Vegas?"

Anna loudly swallowed the lump in her throat, like swallowing a golf ball. She was petrified by Dante's aggression. With her back to the windshield, she opened the passenger door, then she slowly shoved it open. She refused to take her eyes off the hitchhiker. The man was hiding his true intentions, slithering around their questions like a snake in the grass.

Anna asked, "Why wouldn't you want us to call 911? You were attacked, weren't you? We're in danger, right?"

Dante smirked as he leaned forward. He glanced at Austin, then at Anna. With a smug smile plastered on his face, he took a large whiff of the air. He could smell the fear lingering in the vehicle. He closed his eyes and savored the scent. Austin followed his girlfriend's lead, slowly opening his door and preparing his great escape.

With his eyes shut, Dante said, "Maybe I don't want to enter the store and call the cops. Maybe I'm a bank robber trying to escape, maybe I'm a psychopathic serial killer, maybe... maybe..." Dante dramatically paused as he glanced at the generous couple. He beamed from ear-to-ear and said, "Okay, maybe I have absolutely no money to my name and I have a warrant due to unpaid parking tickets. That might be the truth."

Dante chuckled as he leaned back in his seat. He wiped the cold sweat from his brow with the back of his hand and he merrily simpered. He was pleased with his prodding, he loved to build needless tension and stroke fears. Austin and Anna simultaneously sighed in relief.

Anna glared at Dante and said, "That wasn't funny, you–"

Austin interrupted, "Come out with us anyway. I'll pay for everything. You're going to have to face the music for those tickets sooner or later anyway. I'm not a doctor, but I think you'll need one very soon with the blood you've lost."

Dante chuckled, then he said, "Okay, okay. I'm sorry if I scared you. I have a poor sense of humor, I suppose. I'll go with you. Can you give me a hand?"

Anna huffed and crossed her arms as she marched towards the gasoline station. She was not in the mood to play games. Austin glanced back at his frustrated girlfriend and nodded. He wished he could do the same, but he opted to aid the ailing hitchhiker.

***

The door chime echoed through the small store, ringing down the narrow aisles. Austin lent Dante a shoulder, carrying him into the simple filling station. The photographer nodded at the confused cashier, then he led Dante to Anna. Anna stood near a magazine rack next to the entrance, browsing through the collection of printed media. She was immensely irked and frightened, but she veiled her dread with a fabricated nonchalant demeanor.

As the cashier turned his attention to a magazine, Austin said, "Anna, you should go grab something to eat and some drinks for the road. It's still a long trip." He glanced at Dante and said, "Go ahead and find some band-aids and some sutures if they have any. You may be out of luck on that, though. Just find anything you can use. I'll go call for help."

Before he could turn away, Dante grabbed Austin's arm and said, "No, no. You... You go ahead with your girlfriend and grab some food. Grab whatever you need for your trip, handle your business. I should call for help. They were my friends, they're my injuries. I should handle this. Go on. It shouldn't take more than a minute."

Austin gazed into Dante's bloodshot eyes, examining the man's twisted personality. One eye sparkled with sincerity, the other eye spun with deviancy. The hitchhiker wore many masks, changing faces on a whim. The shred of genuine trust Austin harbored in his gullible heart was whisked away with his evaluation, blown out like a candle on a birthday cake.

Dante lurched towards the checkout area. He leaned over the red counter and smirked as he glanced at the young cashier. The young man wore a red polo shirt, black pants, and black work shoes – a simple uniform. He had scruffy brown hair, a muddy mop atop his dome. His brown eyes were kind and welcoming. A plastic badge clung to his chest. The name tag read: *Hello, my name is Chris.*

Chris furrowed his brow and tilted his head like a confused pup. Dante's peculiar leering was mystifying, but the blood was more worrisome. He cared for the well-being of the customer. Yet, the blood dripping onto the counter and white tile flooring was a larger concern at the moment. Cleaning was not a preferred chore for a minimum wage cashier.

Chris grabbed a white rag from the counter behind him and handed it to Dante. He said, "Here. I don't think we have bandages for... for *that.*"

Dante grimaced as he held the rag to his gushing lacerations. He nervously chuckled, then he said, "It must have been a boring day until we showed up, right? I'm sorry about the mess, kid. It's been a long day for me..."

Austin and Anna walked away from the foyer of the shop. Dante's trivial chatter was troublesome, pricking at their logical minds. Something was afoot and the trail was revealing itself with each passing minute. The couple sought refuge at the back of the store, standing between an aisle brimming with junk food and refrigerators filled with bottled water and cheap beer.

Constantly glancing at Dante and Chris, Anna said, "We fucked up, Austin. This is all bad. I mean, he's clearly some sick psychopath. He's... He's... Shit, Austin, we fucked up."

Austin opened the fridge and browsed the bottled water – cheap or expensive, it did not matter. He said, "I know, I know..."

With teary eyes, Anna gazed at the cluttered bags of chips and said, "Those people were murdered. Stabbed and sliced, right? This man... Dante was stabbed in the stomach. I saw the cuts. What if... What if he was the hitchhiker from the story? Hmm? What if we picked up some deranged serial killer?"

"I don't know... I guess it's possible. I swear, someone was sitting in the back seat of that wagon, but I don't know if it was him. I thought it was someone else..."

Slothful, Austin grabbed a generic bottle of water. The photograph in the wagon's sun visor sprung into his mind, vaulting over the dark crevices on his brain. The young, innocent girl was missing in the equation. He couldn't help but ponder the girl's role in the event. *Was she even in the car?*–he thought. He didn't dare bring up the thought to Anna. He didn't want to terrify her any further.

Through the aisle, Anna glared at Dante and said, "Think about it, Austin. We didn't see anyone hitchhiking for miles before or after we found that station wagon. There was no one on the road and I doubt the killer ran into the desert in this weather. No, *he* was the only hitchhiker around." She turned to Austin and said, "We have to leave him. No matter what he says, we can't let him back into the car with us. If you do, then you can leave me here. I swear, I..."

Austin nodded and held his hand up – *please, calm down.* He said, "I understand. I agree with you. We'll leave him here. We'll tell him we're splitting ways. Besides, it'll be better if he waits here for an ambulance and the police. He probably won't try anything with these cameras around, either. We'll leave him behind, okay? *I promise.*"

Anna sniffled and nodded, trying her best to contain her sorrow. She rubbed her eyes with her knuckles, wiping the tears before a waterfall of melancholy could erupt. Her legs wobbled and her body shuddered as she staggered into her boyfriend's arms. She buried her face in his chest and softly whimpered.

Austin stroked her hair and said, "Everything's going to be okay. I promise, everything's going to be fine, sweetheart."

In a muffled tone, Anna said, "I love you."

Staring at Dante with worried eyes, Austin whispered, "I love you, too..."

***

Austin and Anna reluctantly trudged towards the cashier, dragging their feet on the pristine floor. Austin held one water bottle in each hand, Anna gripped two bags of spicy chips in her right hand. The products were inconsequential, though. The grisly day had wiped their appetites. The couple randomly grabbed the food and drinks from the shelves simply to keep some semblance of control.

Dante smirked at the approaching duo. He said, "There you are. Was it busy back there or something? Hell, we were getting ready to send out the search party." His devious cackle caused pain in his mutilated abdomen, but he couldn't help himself. As he recomposed himself, Dante said, "Well, I think we should probably get going now. We've got a long trip ahead of us. Everything's settled, right? You've got your goods?"

Austin furrowed his brow and cocked his head back like a walking pigeon. Dante was clearly jostling his way into the couple's trip. His passive aggressive technique was easily identifiable. On an unassertive person, Dante's method would work perfectly. Austin glanced at the cashier, then back at Dante. He wouldn't allow himself to be steamrolled and manipulated.

Austin said, "Did... Did you call..."

Like if he knew the question before it was asked, Dante interrupted, "Everything's settled on my end, friend. I'll get some bandages at our next stop. This rag should do until then. Let's go ahead and pay for your goods and get this show on the road. Come on." Austin and Anna glanced at each other, nervous. Dante huffed, then he said, "Come on. You have your photography project to get to, right? Let's stop wasting time."

Austin responded, "Listen, we offered you a ride to the nearest stop. We need our privacy, too, okay? Besides, I think you should wait here for an ambulance and the police. You should tell them your story in-person, not some cashier. You were at the..."

With a soul-penetrating stare, Dante glared at Austin and said, "Everything's settled, Austin. *Drop it.*"

With a raised brow, Chris asked, "*Police?* Did you want to use the phone?"

Anna huffed and shook her head, then she sternly said, "You damn liar. I thought everything was settled? What kind of sick game are you trying to play? Huh?"

With a vacant expression, a steady face and absent eyes, Dante glanced at Austin, Anna, and Chris. He huffed, then he burst into a guffaw. The twinge in his stomach did not hurt him. He did not show any signs of pain. Austin and Anna were perturbed by the laughter. Anna sought shelter behind Austin, peeking around his arm for a better view of the madness.

Dante wiped the tears of joy from his face, leaving bloody fingerprints on his cheeks. His smile was wiped with his sudden shift in demeanor – from joyful to menacing within a second. He pulled a switchblade from his back pocket. With the click of a button, the honed blade snapped out of the black handle. His movements were agile, his draw was swift – like a trained gunslinger drawing a revolver from a holster during a duel.

Before Austin and Anna could comprehend the horrifying situation, Dante stabbed the knife into Chris' throat. Wide-eyed, Chris weakly reached for Dante's wrist. As blood jetted from the wound, the young cashier erratically blinked and twitched. Dante pulled the knife out, then he stabbed him again. He did not stop the bloody onslaught. One after the other, the hitchhiker repeatedly stabbed the cashier's throat.

Blood spurted from Chris' neck like a garden sprinkler, dousing Dante with a crimson shower. Holding Chris up with his left hand, the hitchhiker danced in the bloody rain, swinging his hips and shaking his head. With the wag of his index finger, he would have himself an old-fashioned dance. Without stopping his awkward dance, he protruded his tongue and caught the sprinkling blood in his mouth. The pungent taste made his lips quiver with excitement.

Awed, Austin released the bottles of water and

stuttered, "Wha–What... What the fuck? What are you doing?"

Teary-eyed, Anna held her trembling hands to her mouth. She was appalled by the vicious murder. The ferocity of the attack was unexpected. The eccentric dance was uncanny and derisive. 'Shocked' was an understatement. She stood in the presence of a psychopath with few viable options. Only one thought ran through her mind.

Anna gently shoved Austin and whispered, "Run, run, run..." Austin was frozen by his fear. Frustrated and frightened, Anna shouted, "Run!"

Austin tightly shut his eyes and shook his head, snapping out of his trance. He grabbed Anna's hand, forcing her to drop the snacks, then the couple rushed forward. The pair slipped and slid on the bloody floor, barely keeping their balance. Dante snarled like an angry dog as he reached for the pair with his right hand, missing them by a mere fingernail.

Austin and Anna rushed out of the gas station. The pair sprinted to the sedan, fueled by a fear of death. Anna hopped into the passenger seat and locked the door behind her. Austin entered the driver's seat. He tossed his sunglasses on the dashboard and quickly turned the key. Fortunately, the sedan was fairly new. The engine crepitated with the first turn of the key, then it settled to a purr.

Drenched in blood, Dante staggered out of the gasoline station. He shouted, "Wait! You forgot your food! You forgot your drinks!" The wheels squealed as the sedan sped away. Dante chuckled as he watched the absconding couple. He smirked and whispered, "I'll make sure to get it to you in a timely fashion. I'll make sure we see each other again soon..."

Chapter Six

Escaping Insanity

Austin tightly gripped the helm as the vehicle hurtled towards the setting sun. His arms trembled from the dread sitting on his shoulders, causing the car to swerve with each slight movement. He couldn't control his fear and trepidation. He was shocked by the violent attack. The bloody images were engraved into his mind. He could still hear the sound of the young cashier gargling his own blood.

Eyes brimming with tears, Austin whispered, "Why? Why would he kill him like that? What did he do to deserve that? He was just a cashier..." He could not answer the questions for a psychopath – the fact irked him. He stomped on the gas pedal and shouted, "Why? Goddammit, why?!"

Anna sobbed into her hands as she shuddered. She stared out the rear window. The gas station became a mere speck on the glass, shrinking with each passing meter. Although she understood the hitchhiker could not catch them without a car, she could not convince the fear to depart from her mind. She was petrified and logic couldn't smother the feeling.

Glaring down the road ahead, Austin sternly said, "Check your phone. Call the cops. *Now.*"

Anna nodded as she grabbed her cellphone from the floor. The phone slipped and slid out of her hands like a bar of soap in the shower. Her fidgety movements were uncontrollable. Her eyes widened upon spotting the signal symbol at the top of her phone – she was finally connected.

Anna shouted, "I have signal!"

Without easing off the pedal, Austin said, "Call them. Hurry."

Anna quickly dialed 911. Her fingers bounced and trembled with each tap of the screen. With tears streaming down her blushed cheeks, she smiled from ear-to-ear. Relief was an overwhelming sensation. She could feel her body tingling from head-to-toe, like if an army of ants were marching across her skin.

A female operator answered, "911, what is your emergency?"

Anna said, "We just witnessed a murder at a gasoline station. It was the..." Anna glanced at her phone, realizing the call disconnected. She shouted, "Damn it!"

Austin glanced over at his girlfriend and asked, "What? What happened?"

"What the hell do you mean 'what happened?' The damn call disconnected!"

"Try again!"

The wheels howled as the sedan swerved. Austin was struggling to control the vehicle. He was losing control of his vessel and his mind. His jitters were uncontrollable, his anxiety was blatant. Anna wiped the sweat from her brow, then she wrestled with her seat belt. She wasn't going to go down with the ship – even if her captain went down with her.

With one hand on the ceiling, Anna shouted, "Slow down! You're going to kill us! Slow down, Austin!"

Austin shook his head, refusing to budge like a staunch politician. His foot remained firmly planted on the gas pedal despite his girlfriend's request. He understood the dangers of the road. Yet, he feared a madman with a knife and a bizarre taste for blood more than the pavement. He was speeding ahead, placing miles between the couple and the hitchhiker. He was running from murder and chasing death.

Austin huffed, then he said, "I'm not slowing down..."

Anna yelled, "You'll kill us, Austin! I lost signal because you're driving so damn fast! Please, slow down!"

"I'll–I'll slow down, sure. Just give me a minute. Just one minute. I can't let him catch us, Anna, I can't let that happen to you. We have to get as far away from him as possible. You know it. Just give me one more minute, another mile or two. Please..."

Anna withdrew from the argument, like a turtle hiding in its shell. Behind or ahead, the path was fraught with danger. Like her boyfriend, she feared a brutal death more than a car accident. She was distraught by the situation, but she allowed the minute to elapse. As the seconds passed, the couple were awed to see a black car driving towards them in the oncoming lane.

Austin whispered, "Civilization..."

Anna was at a lost for words. She glanced over her shoulder, gazing at the passing car. Her eyes widened as a white truck drove down the oncoming lane – two vehicles within a mile. The sight was welcomed with open arms. She couldn't help but chuckle as she planted her palm on her brow. Austin shared the relief, smiling as he slowed the car and glanced at the side-view mirror.

Anna tapped her phone and said, "I have signal. Keep her steady, sweetie."

A female operator answered, "911, what is your emergency?"

Anxious, Anna responded, "He–Hello. We... we need help. We just witnessed a murder at a gasoline station."

The operator asked, "You witnessed a murder? Okay... Are you at a safe location now, ma'am?"

"Yes, yes. We–We're in our car right now. We're driving away."

"Okay. What gasoline station exactly?"

Anna turned towards Austin and asked, "Where the hell are we?"

Austin responded, "Tell them it was Otto's Gas Station on Route 15."

Relaying the information, Anna said, "It was Otto's Gas Station. It was in the actual store."

The operator said, "Okay. We know the place. Can you describe the suspect and the victim?"

"The man... The *killer* said his name was Dante. We picked him up while he was hitchhiking, so I don't think he has a car. He was bleeding, too. He was tall and... and he had a beard. We also found a station wagon off the side of the road before Otto's Gas Station. There were more dead people inside... I think he killed–"

The operator interrupted, "Okay, ma'am, I need you to listen to me. I'm going to have a state trooper head out to Otto's Gasoline Station. Which direction are you headed now?"

"We're going... north."

"Okay. In that case, you'll be reaching a small diner soon if you haven't passed it already. If you are not in any immediate danger, I would like you to stop there and wait for another officer. You understand? Although other officers will be patrolling and checking up, I'd like you to tell this officer everything in vivid detail. He'll be able to assist you more than I can at this moment."

Anna sniffled, then she said, "Okay."

The operator said, "And remember, ma'am, making a false police report is against the law."

Anna shook her head and responded, "No, I'm not lying to you. He killed–"

Before she could finish, the call disconnected. Disappointed, Anna placed the phone on her thighs and stared down at her boots. She was despondent and dispirited. Austin rubbed her shoulder, gently kneading her skin like dough at a pizza shop.

Austin asked, "What happened?"

Anna responded, "The call disconnected again. The signal on these phones is *crap*. We... We have to cancel our service. We deserve better than this. We deserve to live with a sense of security, not doubt and uncertainty... Shitty phone service... Every time there's a damn killer on the loose, crappy phone service has to get in the way."

Austin stared at his girlfriend with a furrowed brow. Her speech against modern phone companies was peculiar. He agreed, but the statement was irrelevant. His girlfriend was lost in a labyrinthine mind, searching for an escape in an endless tunnel. She was rambling, babbling any thought running through her addled brain.

Austin asked, "What did they say, Anna?"

Anna shook her head, emerging from the twisted maze. She said, "She wants us to stop at a diner. She said a state trooper will meet us there and he'll take our story. She probably thinks we're batshit crazy or something. I don't blame her, I guess."

"The only batshit person around here is Dante. When they find the bodies in the station wagon, when they see the security footage at the gas station, they'll believe everything. I know it. Even if they believe we're crazy, we got through to them. We did it."

Anna whispered, "You're right..."

A structure emerged on the right side of the road, growing as the couple approached. The truck-stop diner glowed like a beacon in hell, illuminated with neon lights like Vegas at night. There were three semi-trucks parked beside the small diner. The eatery was not bustling with customers, but there were enough people around to feel safe.

Anna nodded and said, "That must be it. We just have to wait and see. Maybe we can use their phone and reconnect to the operator. At least it's something, right?"

Austin clenched his jaw, then he said, "State

troopers have to be swarming the interstate, Anna. They have to be getting close. We'll be safe here..."

Chapter Seven

The Diner

Austin and Anna held hands, fingers interlocked like lock and key. Austin inhaled deeply, then he shoved the door open. The door chime reverberated through the diner, bouncing off the white linoleum flooring and brown walls. The ringer was a tocsin of the past, a reminder of the bloody gasoline station massacre. Austin shut his eyes and shuddered, trying his damnedest to shrug off the shrill sound. The pair walked into the diner, then they stopped at the foyer.

The door slowly closed behind them, sealing them in a safe haven. Two men sat at the bar directly ahead, bickering over coffee and dessert. Two truckers filled two separate booths to the right, one trucker filled a booth to the left – munching and slurping. Standing beside the cash register, a cordial waitress waved at the couple from behind the bar.

The middle-aged woman appeared amiable and exhausted – working double jobs surely took a toll, but she kept a smile on her face. She stood a short five-one, curvaceous like Lombard Street. Her blonde hair, clearly dyed, was tied in a tousled bun; a black pen protruded from the bundle of hair. She wore a blue a-line dress with a white collar and shoulder-length sleeves. In cursive writing, the name tag on her chest read: *Patricia.* The diner had an old-fashioned vibe and she complemented it perfectly.

Austin nodded at the waitress, then he shambled towards the farthest corner to the left. Anna followed closely, trusting her boyfriend's judgment. She wanted to keep a safe distance from the entrance. Austin shared the same thought, but he also wanted a clear view of the parking lot – a strategic vantage point. The potential of a surprise visit from Dante kept him on the edge.

Austin flumped into the crimson padded seat of the final booth on the left. Anna sat directly across from him with her back to the trucker residing in the neighboring booth. Said trucker sipped his coffee, loud and proud, while shuffling through a rustling newspaper. The hulking man was fairly simple. He had wild brown hair, a thick beard, and black bags under his eyes. Nothing out of the ordinary.

As she stared into the parking lot, Anna asked, "How long do you think it'll take them to get here? They can't be far, right?"

Austin stared down the opposite side of the road, vigilant. He responded, "I don't know. I just hope it doesn't take them too long. I know they told us to wait here, but it doesn't feel great stopping. He could be coming for us..."

Disrupting the doleful mood, Patricia approached the booth and ecstatically said, "Welcome to *Drifter's Diner.* Would you like to hear today's specials? Or are you ready to order?"

Austin responded, "You know, I don't think we'll

be eating tonight. We're only waiting for the police, then we'll be out of your hair."

Patricia furrowed her brow and repeated, "The police?"

"Yeah. We were told to wait here for a state trooper, I guess. We have to fill him in on a... a crime, I suppose. We won't be ordering anything tonight. Thank you, Patricia."

Patricia puckered her lips and nodded, intrigued. She straggled away without saying another word, constantly glancing over her shoulder. As Austin and Anna turned their attention to the parking lot, the neighboring trucker took a gander at the pair. He neatly folded his newspaper, then he loudly coughed – an attention grabber.

The trucker said, "Hey, buddy, did you say you were waiting for the police?"

Austin and Anna glanced at the trucker, baffled by the man's prying. Like deer caught in the headlights, the pair could not answer or move. They were caught off guard. The couple shared the same thought: *why does he want to know?*

Austin nodded and said, "Yeah. That's what I said. We're waiting for the police."

As he caught a glimpse of the fear in Anna's eyes, the trucker chuckled. He said, "I'm sorry. That was rude of me, wasn't it? Eavesdropping, questioning... Forgive my poor manners. I was taught better than that. My name is Trevor. I'm... I stop here very often, going back-and-forth and all, and I usually don't see people waiting for cops at diners. It just caught my attention."

Anna bit her bottom lip, then she said, "Well, we had a little 'run-in' with a hitchhiker and I'm afraid it turned out a bit violent. Sorry if we seem a bit suspicious about everything. It's no offense to you, but you probably haven't seen what we've seen."

In a dubious tone, Trevor whispered, "A hitchhiker?" He was bothered by the simple word, perturbed by the concept. He pointed at the couple's booth and asked, "You mind if I join you? You're probably scared now, I know, but maybe it'll help if you talk about it. To be honest, you *really* caught my attention with all this hitchhiker and police talk now. Do you mind?"

Austin and Anna stared at each other, communicating without words. Their eyes spoke volumes about the situation. Fear lingered in their pupils, but the dread dwindled with the security of the environment. The trucker did not seem malicious, either. The couple nodded in agreement – *sure*.

As Anna moved to her boyfriend's side, Austin said, "Come on over."

***

Trevor planted his coffee mug on the table, then he sat across the distraught couple. He loudly yawned and stretched as he shuffled in the comfortable seat. The sweet allure of sleep was baiting him, inviting him to slumber. Despite his heavy eyelids, the exhausted trucker stayed awake. Curiosity kept him conscious.

Trevor licked his lips, then he said, "So, tell me about the hitchhiker. You can tell me about what you experienced, sure, but tell me about the man. Describe him to me, if it's not asking too much. He was a man, right?"

Austin nodded and said, "Yeah, a man. He was... Hell, I don't know what to say. He–He looked normal, you know? He had black hair and a beard. A little slim, I guess. He said his name was Dante. I don't know what else to say. He wasn't anything... *special,* I guess."

"Okay, okay. And, what did this fella do to warrant a call to the police?"

Chiming-in, Anna said, "We saw him *kill* a man and I'm pretty damn sure he killed two more people in a station wagon. He's... He's one of those psycho hitchhikers you used to see on the news or the ones you heard about in urban legends. *A fucking maniac.* I think that warrants a call to the police. If you ask me, I think it warrants a goddamn death sentence. And, frankly, I don't give a crap if you or the police don't believe me. We know what we saw."

Wide-eyed, Trevor gazed at the fiery young woman. Her sharp tongue stabbed his lethargic demeanor – a wake-up call. Austin stared at his girlfriend with narrowed eyes, then he glanced around the eatery. With the fierce speech, the patrons and staff inconspicuously glanced towards the commotion from the corner of their eyes. A nosy audience surrounded them. Austin simply waved at the spectators – *go back to your regularly scheduled program, people.*

Trevor sniffled, then he said, "I see. In that case, I agree with you, ma'am. You are correct. In a sense, though, you're lucky. You're *very* lucky. Hell, if those people are really dead, then they're lucky, too. They've already escaped. Count your blessings, ma'am, at least you didn't run into the other one..."

Anna furrowed her brow and repeated, "*The other one?*"

Baffled, Austin asked, "Who the hell is 'the other one?' Do you know Dante?"

Trevor inhaled deeply, then he loudly sighed. He explained, "The other one... The other one is a thing of superstition around these parts. Like you said, ma'am, a thing of 'urban legend.' For years, there's been a very violent problem with hitchhiker's on this interstate. That's why you *never* pick up a hitchhiker. *Never.* It doesn't matter if he's injured or sick, or if he looks innocent or if she looks pretty, you never pick up a hitchhiker..."

Austin swallowed the lump in his throat, then he asked, "Why?"

"Well, around these parts, *they'll butcher you.* I'm sorry if it sounds crass, but I'm just being blunt. This boy, Dante, I'm sure I've seen him before on the road, trying to wave down some gullible drivers and trying to convince them to pick him up. His brother... Well, his brother is a different story. His brother is the reason they call this place 'Butcher Road.' He's the reason behind this road's reputation. I'm sure of it."

Anna leaned closer and asked, "Are you telling us Dante has a brother? You're saying there's more than one killer on this interstate?" She leaned back in her seat, awed by the story. She whispered,

"*Butcher Road...* Unbelievable..."

Trevor knocked on the table – three thuds to get their attention. He explained, "Now, like I said, this is something of an urban legend. I heard about these two guys a few years ago. One time, I heard about them walking down the interstate with decapitated heads clenched in their hands, smiling at the passing drivers. *Real heads.* I heard about violent attacks and kidnappings, all blamed on the same brothers. With all of this talk of grave-robbing and human trafficking on the news, I'm inclined to believe this legend is real. At least, somewhat real. So, I never pick up a hitchhiker. I would never take a risk like that. You'd have to be a dumb–"

Trevor stopped and bit his bottom lip. He was not in the business of insulting kind patrons. He caught himself before his language slipped from welcoming to vulgar. Austin and Anna glanced at each other with uncertain eyes – the lingering fear never departed. The trucker spun a yarn like if he were telling a horror story around a campfire.

"What do you know about Dante's brother?" Austin asked.

Trevor nodded and said, "Well, for one, I believe his name is *Clyde.* Dante and Clyde, the interstate butchers. I heard Clyde is a ruthless man. He's much worse than Dante. He's... He's not the handsome-type, either. He's a big boy with some sort of skin disease, I think. I call him a 'boy' because I heard he acts like a child. You'll know when you see him. Yeah, you'll know... At least, that's what I've heard." As Patricia walked by, Trevor waved at the waitress and said, "Hey, Patricia, can you bring some coffee for these two? The blacker, the better. They're going to need it."

Patricia smiled and nodded, imperturbable. The woman was genuinely happy to serve her patrons. Although she could overhear the bits and pieces of the disturbing conversation, she was more than willing to offer a helping hand.

Patricia strolled towards the bar and shouted, "It'll be on the house."

Disregarding the cordial waitress, Austin asked, "What do you mean by that, Trevor? 'They're going to need it.' What the hell is that supposed to mean?"

Trevor responded, "Just 'cause you got away, that doesn't mean you 'got away.' Think about it. If all of this urban legend crap is true, then you saw one of them. You saw *one* of the butcher brothers. You should be speeding home, not wasting time here."

"We're not going to run off in the dark. We're waiting here for the police," Anna said.

"Unfortunately, the police can't help you if those boys get to you first. You should be going towards them. You should be heading into the next town, not waiting here to get caught up in a bloody mess. You understand?"

The trucker's analysis wasn't wrong. The couple had a set of viable options on the table: wait, hide, or run. Each option had advantages and disadvantages. The psychopathic hitchhikers, on the other hand, would not waste time making their decision – kill, kill, *kill.* Austin and Anna sat in silence, contemplating their strategy.

Trevor stood up and said, "Listen, you go ahead and do whatever you like. I'm going to enjoy my pie and my coffee. I hate to say this, but... I didn't see or hear anything. I'm blind and deaf for the rest of the night. Good luck."

***

Trevor grunted and groaned as he slipped into his booth. He sipped his coffee, loudly slurping the scorching liquid. Without a glance at the overwrought couple, he lifted the rustling newspaper and covered his view. He offered his knowledge on the area, he offered some advice. He was done with the situation.

Patricia walked towards the despondent duo, her white sneakers thudding on the floor with each step. She placed two white ceramic mugs on the table, then she bowed. The pair were blatantly distressed by their horrific day and she did not want to aggravate the problem. She didn't need a 'thank you' to fuel her helpful personality anyway.

Austin scooted towards the window and peered towards the parking lot. He asked, "What do you think we should do? You want to drive to the next stop or wait?"

Anna responded, "I know it can be dangerous, but I think we should wait. I think it's the most logical thing to do. The cops told us to wait here, so we should *wait here.* These people won't let anything happen to us, right? They won't just stand there and let some madman attack us. It's four, five people against one or two."

"It all sounds good on paper, but I'm not too sure

about that. I don't think these truckers want anything to do with us or Dante. It doesn't sound like they want anything to do with the 'other one.' We can only wait and see."

With brooding eyes, Austin stared at the road. A vehicle drove down the narrow road every five minutes. There wasn't a single new customer since their arrival. The remote diner seemed exclusive to truckers – an afterthought to the world, or not a thought at all. The photographer could only think about Trevor's ominous warning and his fearful retreat.

Austin said, "Maybe we should just go. We can head straight to Vegas. No more stops. We'll report everything there. At least we'll be surrounded by thousands of people out there. We'll be in a city that never sleeps. A thousand against one or two, those are much better odds."

With a pinch of resentment, Anna responded, "That... That doesn't sound like a good idea, Austin. Not with Dante out there. If he really has a brother, they're probably looking for us now. He wouldn't have to walk to catch up."

"If he doesn't have to walk, then he's probably already coming this way. There are only two ways on this road, Anna, and we're sitting in the middle. We're sitting here waiting for a cop that's probably on a damn doughnut break. Let's get the hell out of here."

Anna uttered a mere croak of a word – a letter. She stared out the window, frightened. Austin turned his attention to the parking lot. His jaw dangled from the utter shock. A figure shambled down the road, limping towards the roadside diner. Although the person could not be seen through the darkness, their imaginations were fueled by sheer terror.

Anna stuttered, "Is–Is it... Is it him? A–Austin..."

Austin clenched his fists and glared at the lumbering figure. His breathing intensified with each slow step. He thought about running into the kitchen and grabbing a chef's knife to defend himself. He even considered using the scorching coffee as a weapon. Before he could decide, the person stepped into the diner's light. The everyday man walked past the eatery. He did not resemble Dante and he was not large like his supposed brother. The couple shared a sigh of relief.

As Austin took a swig of his coffee, Anna tugged on his arm and said, "Fine. Let's get the hell out of here."

Chapter Eight

Running from Murder

The sedan whizzed down the desolate road, led to safety by the dazzling headlights. An impenetrable darkness swallowed the desert area, like if a bank of black fog were billowing over the region. The ominous shadows were accompanied by a frigid cold. The weather plummeted with the falling sun. The nippy conditions even seeped into the car.

A driver sped down the oncoming lane every other minute. Aside from the brief company, silence reigned supreme. As the oncoming drivers became more sparse, spread out for miles, the loneliness became evident. The forsaken sensation was eerie. The world was whisked away, unaware of the horror lurking on the interstate.

Breaking the silence, Anna asked, "Do you really think this is a good idea?" She glanced out her window, saddened. She said, "I'm just so confused. I don't know what to do."

Austin nodded, keeping his slimy hands on the steering wheel. He explained, "We waited at that diner for a while and no one showed up. We've been driving for a few minutes and we still haven't seen a single cop coming our way. It's almost like they forgot about us. I mean, how far apart are these state troopers? You'd figure they'd be speeding down to a homicide, right? It's just... It's just not worth waiting for that man to catch up. If he's as psycho as the trucker says, we might as well put up a fight... Well, I guess we're actually running, but at least it's something."

"I'm sorry for being so... so dramatic back there. I don't know about all of this. I'm scared. I'm scared and I'm tired. That's all."

"I know, I know. To be honest with you, I'm scared, too."

Anna huffed and smirked. She couldn't help herself. She saw a golden opportunity and she had to seize it. She wanted to inject some humor into the dreadful situation, she wanted to unleash her exuberance to brighten the mood. The despairing circumstances were vexing and humor was a common remedy for sorrow.

In a blatantly sarcastic tone, Anna said, "No, really?"

Austin nervously chuckled – he appreciated the snark. He said, "Yeah, I'm a *little* scared. I'll get through it, though, I always do."

"*We'll* get through it together. How long do you think it'll be until we see a town or a cop? Or Vegas? That would be like finding heaven in hell, right? Imagine that. Leaving a sinful man for Sin City, very strange..."

"We should start seeing more businesses coming up soon. Maybe a small town. You know, somewhere to stop and rest. There's not going to be a single gas station and a diner in the middle of nowhere. No, we'll see something soon. I'm positive."

Anna nodded in agreement. She turned back in

her seat and stared out the rear window. She could not see anything through the gloomy darkness. There were no following vehicles in sight, no headlights or squealing wheels. The long and seemingly endless road was abandoned. The couple were more likely to see the headlights of a phantom car than an actual driver.

Anna asked, "Are you tired? Can you keep driving?"

Austin sighed, then he said, "I had a sip of coffee. It wasn't much, but I think I'll be fine. How about you?"

"Yeah. I'm exhausted. I'm tired of... of all of this. I'm just so damn sick and tired of today. I wish it would just end."

"Maybe you should try getting some rest. I should have got the cable out for you when we were at the diner. I know you like sleeping with music. I'm sorry about that."

Anna smiled and nodded, temporarily relaxed by her boyfriend's thoughtful apology. She whispered, "It's okay, sweetie. It's fine."

Anna turned back into her seat, wrestling with her seat belt. She stared at the beams of light emitting from their sedan. The light was minuscule compared to the sprawling desert, but the illumination was undoubtedly heartening – a flare in an endless pit of darkness. The young college student closed her eyes and pondered the horrifying situation. A gruesome death echoed through her pessimistic mind. Her appalling thoughts of terror led her to a single escape route – *sleep.*

***

Anna loudly gasped, awakened by a blaring horn. The vehicle violently jounced, shaking and swerving uncontrollably. Austin wrestled with the steering wheel as he glanced over his shoulder. Following suit, Anna stared out the rear window with wide eyes. A large cherry-red pickup truck rammed the sedan from behind.

Over the obnoxious horn, Anna yelled, "What the hell is he doing?! He's going to kill us!"

Anna sobbed into her hands as she hopelessly tried to tame her anxiety. Her fretful whimpers reflected the frenzied attack. Austin could hear the plaintive cries, but he was only concerned with keeping control of the vehicle and surviving. He swerved as he tried to avoid dropping into a ditch like the station wagon. He refused to experience the same fate as the slaughtered couple.

The truck slowed down for a few seconds, then it quickly accelerated. The reckless driver cycled between two speeds, purposely ramming into the sedan over and over. The driver's pattern of attack was easily recognizable. The several collisions were not accidental and he was not trying to hide his intentions. Murder was the goal. The reasoning behind the attack, however, was unknown.

As he tightly gripped the steering wheel, Austin glanced at Anna and sternly asked, "Is it him?! Anna, is it him? Is it Dante?"

Anna wiped the tears from her blushed cheeks as she reluctantly glanced back at the pursuing truck. She narrowed her teary eyes, trying to clear her blurred vision. She did not recognize the driver. Their chaser appeared as a giant silhouette in the truck. Despite the obtrusive darkness, she could see the figure was too large to be Dante. Anna shook her head and shuddered.

With a quivering lip, she stuttered, "N–No... I–I don't think it's him. He's... He's too big, Austin. That's not Dante..." With wide eyes, she glanced at her boyfriend and asked, "Can it... Can it be 'the other one?' Is it his brother?"

Flustered by the pursuit, Austin yelled, "I don't know, damn it! I don't know!"

The couple swayed in their seats, tossed every which way by another violent collision. The wheels squealed with the frantic swerve. The crazed driver in the truck blared his horn, pressing down on his steering wheel without a single pause. The ruckus conjured by the chase created a cacophonous symphony of hectic noise. The desolate desert was dominated by chaos. As the truck slowed down, Austin seized the opportunity to roll his window down.

Anna sank into her seat and tightly shut her eyes. She planted her palms over her ears, but the makeshift plugs could not block the madness. The racket was too loud. Although she did not physically abandon her boyfriend, she mentally attempted to depart the vehicle – whisked away with thoughts of nothingness.

Austin protruded his head from the window and shouted, "Go around! Go around!" He wanted to believe the confrontation was nothing more than a misunderstanding – an angry driver trying to get ahead. With a vein bulging down the center of his brow, Austin yelled, "Please, go around! We didn't do anything! *Go around!*"

The thunderous roar of the accelerating truck echoed through the desert like a lion's roar in Africa. The deafening sound sent chills down Austin's spine. The crepitating engine was unusually daunting. The everyday noise rattled his core. Before he could maneuver and prepare himself, the truck rammed the back of the sedan at a breakneck speed.

Austin stomped on the brakes as the car rolled off the road. The car bounced on the pitted ground until it finally stopped. Particles of dirt filled the air around the vehicle, majestically swaying back to the ground. Frightened, Austin glanced back at the road. The pursuing truck hurtled down the road without a brake or swerve.

Breathing heavily, Austin turned towards Anna and asked, "Are you okay, sweetie? Are you hurt? Huh? *Are you hurt?*"

Anna slowly blinked as she rubbed the nape of her neck. The force of the sudden stop whiplashed her head. She held her other hand to her chest. Each heartbeat was rapid, echoing through her entire body. She could hear the thumping palpitations thrumming in her ears. The young woman was discomfited.

Anna said, "I... I think I'm okay. I think–" She gazed into Austin's eyes, then she sobbed into her hands. In a slur of words, she said, "I... I don't know... I didn't... What... What the hell did he want? Why...

Why did he do this to us, Austin? What did we do?"

Austin caressed her hair and softly shushed. He said, "Don't cry, Anna. Please, don't cry." He examined her neck and her face, searching for any visible wounds. Fear seemed to be her ultimate ailment. Austin said, "Listen, I think you're okay. You're fine, sweetheart. You just wait here and rest. Recompose yourself, okay? I'm going to make sure he's gone. Wait here."

Anna grabbed Austin's forearm. With wide eyes, she asked, "You're going out there?"

"I have to. I have to make sure he's really gone. Just wait here. I'll be right back."

Anna leaned back in her seat and stuttered, "O–Okay..."

Austin slowly exited the vehicle. His legs wobbled with his first few steps, like if his limbs changed into noodles during the crash. The anxiety and fear blending in his body concocted a formula of uncontrollable giddiness. With his limp legs, he trudged towards the road. The photographer narrowed his eyes as he stared down the interstate. He couldn't see a single car light and the racket from the engine vanished.

He whispered, "He's gone... Who are you? What do you want from us?" Dejected, he shook his head and kicked at the pebbles on the road. He muttered, "Damn it..."

Austin hopped as he felt a moist hand grab his wrist. Wide-eyed, he stared back at the source, then he sighed in relief. Anna, disconsolate and scared, stood behind Austin and tugged on her boyfriend's arm. She wanted to withdraw from the front-lines and retreat back to their vehicle. She shuddered from the fear and frigid conditions, but she refused to release Austin's arm.

Anna said, "Come on. Let's go back to the car. There's nothing for us out here."

Austin opened his mouth to respond, then he stopped. He furrowed his brow as he stared into Anna's lusterless eyes. Anna was baffled by his erratic behavior, tilting her head like a confused pup. Austin glanced over his shoulder, staring down the truck's getaway route. He weaved and bobbed his head for a better view, like if the motions would help him see through the pitch-black night. He could see a set of lights approaching from afar – white specks on a black canvas.

Austin said, "Someone's coming..."

Chapter Nine

A Glimmer in the Darkness

Austin and Anna staggered back towards the sedan, shocked and horrified. The thought running through their minds was the same: *he's coming back to finish the job.* Anna lurched towards their car until she tumbled near the trunk. Austin stood at the side of the road, paralyzed by his fear. His fight-or-flight response caused him to freeze. He found himself trapped in the center; his body wanted to grapple, his mind wanted to run.

As she crawled in reverse, Anna shouted, "Austin! What are you doing?! What are you waiting for?!" Austin did not respond – his vocabulary was wiped like an extinct language. Anna sniveled as she said, "Please... Austin..."

As the headlights approached, Austin shuddered and slowly shook his head. His imagination ran wild, leading him to believe a hearse from Hell was approaching to pick him up. To his utter surprise, the approaching vehicle was more like a chariot from Heaven. A black police cruiser with a yellow stripe across the side rolled to a stop next to the crash site.

Austin turned towards Anna and said, "It's the police... It's the police, Anna. It's the damn highway patrol!"

Anna nervously chuckled as she staggered to her

feet. She had never been happier to meet an officer of the law – a doting guardian angel. She was rendered speechless by her overwhelming relief. She could only smile as she sauntered to Austin's side. She watched as a state trooper stepped out of the police cruiser.

The burly man stood a respectable six-one. He had a shaved dome and glistering blue eyes. He wore a standard police uniform – a dark navy shirt, navy trousers, a utility belt, and black insulated boots. A badge and an embroidered tag dangled from his chest. The name tag read: *S. Anderson.* The officer seemed stern but kind.

Anderson sniffled, then he approached the couple. He said, "You seem to have dropped yourselves into a little problem. You guys need any assistance? Or do you have it all handled?"

Austin frantically waved, then he said, "I know we're going to sound crazy, officer, but please listen to us. We were... We were *chased* off the road by some madman! He rammed us with his truck! A... A *red* truck. He killed someone, too. I mean, we *think* it was the same guy who killed the cashier at the gas station and that couple over at the other accident. He's... He's killing everyone on this goddamn road."

Anderson furrowed his brow, overwhelmed by the copious amount of information gyrating into his ears. He said, "Alright, slow down. Take a deep breath, young man. What exactly are you talking about here?"

Sniffling with tears streaming down her cheeks, Anna said, "We called you once already. We reported this man for killing the cashier at... at Otto's Gas Station or something like that. You must have heard something about it. The lady, the operator, she said you'd meet us at the diner. *Please,* tell me you can help us. *Please.*"

Anderson raised his brow as he examined the distraught couple and the scene. A small crash, a few bruises, plenty of tears, and shared hysteria painted a suspicious portrait. *Drugs, alcohol, insanity, or all of the above,* he thought. Before he could blurt out an accusation, the officer's eyes widened – an epiphany.

Anderson smiled and whispered, "The diner... Shit..." He turned his attention to the couple and said, "Okay, let's just step back and try to relax. I understand the situation. Well, I know what you're talking about. You're the ones that called in the accident and the gas station robbery?"

Anna stomped and shouted, "It wasn't a robbery, it was a murder!"

"Okay, okay. Calm down, miss. We received the call, but we've had a busy night. There might have been some miscommunication along the way, too. I apologize for that. We should have an officer moving up to the crash site soon. You said it was a few miles before the station, right?"

Austin nodded and said, "Yeah."

"Well, in that case, he should be there any minute now. In fact, he's probably there now. So, I'm going to grab a flare from my car, okay? I'll come back and get the rest of your story in a minute. Are both of you okay? Do you need any medical assistance?"

Austin and Anna glanced at each other. The pair

were bothered by the day and bruised by the crash, but they did not require an ambulance. The resilient duo could trudge through the aches and saunter towards safety without paramedics. With the police officer's presence, at least the pair found some solace and security.

Austin said, "We're fine."

Anderson retrieved a road flare from his trunk. He struck the coarse surface of the cap on the flare, like if he were lighting a match to smoke a cigarette. The flare illuminated the area with a vibrant red glow, vanishing the shadows. He tossed the flare on the ground to warn other drivers, then he turned his attention to Austin and Anna.

Anderson said, "I have a few questions for you two. First and foremost, do you have any weapons on you?" Austin and Anna shook their heads. Anderson nodded and said, "Good. Have you been drinking tonight? Did you take any drugs? Marijuana? Cocaine? Heroin? Or–"

Austin interrupted, "We don't have any guns and we don't do drugs. Why are you treating us like criminals? We witnessed a murder. I'd think that would be at the top of your priorities. I mean, the guy is getting away as we speak. You probably drove right past him."

"It's only procedure. I don't know if you're armed or if you're hopped up on drugs. Secondly, you said a red truck rammed you off the road. I didn't see a truck coming down by here for miles. So, although we are investigating your *very* serious claims, we have to approach this from every angle. Now, do you mind if I check the vehicle for any drugs or weapons?"

Anna huffed and rolled her eyes, then she said, "You can check all you want, but you'd just be wasting your time."

Anderson smiled and said, "Thank you, miss. We'll get to your–"

Anderson was interrupted by his radio. He lifted his index finger to the couple – *one moment, please.* The officer stepped towards the trunk, holding the radio on his chest. He indistinctly murmured as he kept his eyes locked on Austin and Anna. He was vigilant. The pair could hear bits and pieces of the quiet conversation from afar, but not nearly enough. Austin stepped closer, Anna followed his lead.

Over the radio, a male officer said, "I'm at the gas station now, Anderson. There was no station wagon back on the road and Otto's is closed right now. I've called Hank to see what's going on. I'm sure this place should be open now. Other than that, there doesn't seem to be anything else wrong around here. I have no signs of a 187 anywhere."

Anderson responded, "10-4. I may have a 5150 in my hands, possibly a–"

Confounded by the officer's response, Austin shouted, "I swear, that man slaughtered the cashier! He killed those people in the station wagon! He slaughtered them! We're not crazy! *We're not crazy!*"

Anderson held his hands up in a peaceful gesture, calling for silence. He said, "Calm down, sir. We're investigating–"

Anna interrupted, "You're not investigating! You

think we're stupid! You think we're crazy, don't you? *5150?* We know what it means. We're not crazy." She sobbed as she staggered back, contemplating an explanation – searching for a missing detail. As a bulb illuminated above her head, Anna said, "Go... Go back and ask the truckers. Go to the diner and ask the truckers. They know all about this man and his killing spree. There's a psycho out here trying to kill us, officer. Please, believe me..."

Austere, Anderson sternly said, "Alright, that's enough. Look, I'll get you off this road. I'll take you down to the closest station or checkpoint. We'll get this sorted out there. Does that sound good to you?"

Austin lifted his arm and stepped in reverse, gently pushing Anna back. He didn't trust the police officer. '5150,' a code for mentally disturbed people, clung to his mind. Under the circumstances, entering the backseat of the police cruiser was like buying a ticket to jail. He refused to sell his freedom for an uncertain trade.

Austin said, "If you really believe us, if you really want to take us to safety, you'll let us follow you there in our car. We're not wearing your handcuffs and we're not getting into the backseat. We'll follow your directions, we'll follow you, but we're *not* getting into your car."

Anderson responded, "No one said anything about handcuffs, sir."

"You didn't have to."

Anderson huffed in disbelief, mystified by the couple's erratic behavior. He furrowed his brow and said, "You see, now you're acting suspicious."

Austin explained, "We... We were told not to trust hitchhikers, but I think that rule applies to you, too."

Anderson chuckled, then he asked, "You don't trust me?"

***

With the milky moonlight washing over their bodies, the trio were caught in a grueling deadlock. Only the whooshing wind sliced through the eerie silence. Anderson sought to take the couple into temporary custody – with or without handcuffs. Austin wanted to keep himself and his girlfriend free to maneuver. He refused to willingly restrain himself with a vicious murderer on the loose.

One hand on his belt, Anderson scratched his eyebrow and shook his head as he approached the apprehensive duo. Austin could see the officer's hand drifting towards the holstered handgun. The state trooper would not draw and shoot without provocation, but he was more than willing to apprehend the couple through force.

Anderson said, "Listen, I don't want to do this the hard way. We can sit here and grapple until I get you into custody or we can wait for backup to arrive, but I'd rather just take you out of here the easy way. Let me pat you down, you hop into my car, then I drive you down to a station. It's that simple. You have my word."

Anna said, "Nothing's that 'simple' around here. We thought picking up a hitchhiker would be *simple* and he turned out to be a maniac. We just want to leave. You understand? We don't want any more trouble. We were heading to Vegas for work, that's all."

"Alright, alright. I get it. So, here's what I can do for you. I'm going to need your cooperation, though. You can get into your car and head north. I'll follow behind you until we hit a checkpoint or until I receive an update. As long as you stay in my headlights, there won't be any problems. Sound good?"

Austin and Anna glanced at each other with deadpan expressions – steady faces of relief. The police officer's offer was sincere and appreciated. He was not as devious as originally imagined. He was simply taking all precautions while on duty – *understandable.* The pair nodded in agreement.

Anderson rubbed his hands together and said, "Great. I still have to pat you down, though. So, let's get this–"

The sound of a sputtering engine disrupted the deal. The roaring grew louder with each passing second, like the rumbling stomach of a starved man amplified tenfold. The booming engine was accompanied by a blaring horn. The vehicular racket rapidly increased in volume. Anderson glanced over Austin's shoulder and tilted his head. He could see the headlights of a truck approaching from afar.

Austin's eyes widened as he recognized the ruckus. He didn't have to look back to know who was approaching. The truck left a permanent imprint on his fractured psyche. The day was already filed under 'unforgettable' in his mind. Anna grimaced as she wept. She recognized the approaching sound of death.

Anderson strolled towards the pair and murmured, "What the hell is this guy doing?"

Austin said, "We have to go."

Anderson glanced at Austin with a furrowed brow and asked, "What?"

"It's a truck, isn't it? We have to go. If it's a red truck, then that's the hitchhiker or his brother. We have to go. We have to get the hell out of here."

Anderson stared at the approaching headlights, mystified. He nodded at the begrimed sedan on the side of the road, motioning his demands – *go on, run.* Austin and Anna watched the valiant officer with narrowed eyes, astonished. The officer moseyed towards danger with his hand on his holster. He walked ahead of the couple, then he drew his handgun. He could see the truck was approaching without any intention to stop.

Anderson whispered, "What the hell are you doing, buddy?" As the truck hurtled towards the crash site, the officer shouted, "Stop! Stop!"

Anderson stepped aside as the truck charged forward. He gritted his teeth and fired three rounds at the truck – one penetrated the windshield, the others missed. The gunfire did not stall the speeding vehicle. The officer attempted to leap out of the way, but he was caught by the truck's massive range. Anderson was tossed five meters into the air like a flimsy rag doll. The truck barreled through him like a wrecking ball smashing through dry wall. The thud and crunching sound reverberated as his body collided with the pavement.

Austin and Anna jumped out of the way, sliding

across the dirt as the truck drove off the road. The couple slipped and slid as they rushed towards their sedan. They could hear the truck skidding to a stop, bouncing on the rutted dirt and driving over the dried shrubs.

Austin turned the key in the ignition, struggling to start the car. Anna locked the doors, then she buckled her seat belt. The belt was supposed to prevent serious accidents, but she had hoped the safety strap would keep her restrained to the seat if she had to fight off a crazed hitchhiker.

Anna frantically tapped Austin's forearm and said, "Hurry, hurry, hurry..."

Frustrated, Austin shouted, "I'm trying!"

Anna stared in shock as a colossal man climbed out of the driver's seat of the truck – *Clyde Hooper.* The figure stood a towering six-seven with a wide frame. The person was clearly heavy. His weight and strength were undeniable. He appeared powerful enough to move mountains with a flick of his finger. With the limited moonlight, she could see the figure had wild hair – strands protruding every which way. The corpulent man held a large tool in his hands – a spear, an ax, *a hammer?*

Another fairly tall figure emerged from the other side of the truck. The man was leaner than the driver. The passenger hobbled beside the larger man, limping towards the road. The slim figure was easily recognizable, even through the darkness. *Dante,* Anna thought, *that must be Dante and his brother.*

As the car engine purred, Austin ecstatically said,

"There!"

The sedan bounced as the photographer heedlessly reversed. He returned to the road, then he sped away from the commotion. As he glanced at the rear-view mirror, he stomped on the brakes. The pair were flung forward from the sudden stop. He sought an escape from the madness, he wanted a head start, but the helpful officer caught his eye.

Anderson writhed in pain on the road. He was not killed upon impact – not by the truck or the pavement. The tough and brave man survived the head-on collision. His handy firearm, however, was lost in the shadows. His only advantage against death was out of arm's reach. The ominous figures from the truck slowly approached, taunting the downed officer. They mocked the helpless man, dancing and spitting around him.

Austin asked, "Should... Should we help him?"

Eyes full of tears, Anna stared out the back window and responded, "It's too late."

Austin nodded and stepped on the gas pedal, reluctantly cruising away from the crime. He didn't glance at the rear-view mirror again. He wanted to save himself and his girlfriend. The couple's survival was his top priority. If he glanced back, he was afraid he'd feel compelled to return to the scene.

Anna stared at the silhouettes from afar, trying to identify the men. The group was illuminated by the neighboring flare, but the savage pursuers shrank with the distance. The young college student could barely see them. However, she could see the burly man lifting a tool over his head – *a sledgehammer, surely.*

The hulking man swung the sledgehammer down at Anderson, striking the center of his forehead with the metal head. Anderson violently convulsed from the savage blow, shaking on the ground like a fish out of water. The large man lifted the sledgehammer over his dome, then he swung down again. The state trooper's skull was crushed. Blood gushed from the lacerations on his dented forehead. His eyeball popped out from its socket, plummeting to the pavement.

Anna shuddered as she witnessed the event. She couldn't see the blood splatter or the head explode, but she could see Anderson's trembling body and each strike. The silhouettes spoke volumes about the attack. The men were barbaric, celebrating the cruel killing. Anna sat forward in her seat, lost in her thoughts. She wondered: *could he have survived with our help?* The officer was left for dead, sacrificed for the pair's survival. The couple did not share another word on the matter.

Chapter Ten

The Motel

Anna stared out the back window, keeping her eyes locked on the road behind the sedan. The road was desolate, lonely and eerie. Although the couple had traveled a dozen miles from the crash site, she still believed the sinister men could catch up to them in an instant. The wicked brothers were not hindered by a fear of death, speed was merely an adrenaline rush.

Wide-eyed, Austin said, "Anna, look..."

Anna reluctantly turned in her seat, afraid she might find another grisly accident. She was surprised to see two buildings on the right side of the road. The lonesome buildings were illuminated, welcoming stragglers from far and wide. The first structure was a diner, the neighboring building was a motel. The tantalizing scent of roadside delicacies and the sweet allure of sleep called their names, seductively whispering into their ears with honeyed words. *Grab a bite, get some sleep.*

Austin asked, "Should we stop?"

As they approached, Anna stared at the buildings and said, "I'm not sure. It might not be a good idea."

"I don't think I can keep going. I'm... I know you think it's a joke, but I'm scared and I'm tired. I need some rest. If I keep going, I'm afraid I'm going to crash and get us killed. They'll catch up to us anyway, won't they? They're faster than us, they're more reckless. They won't give up."

Anna glanced at her boyfriend with vacant eyes. She was equally exhausted and afraid, but she had already drained all of her tears. She could not cry. She scrunched her face as she recognized the fear in her boyfriend's voice. She understood the hopeless dilemma. One way or another, the persistent brothers would find them and slaughter them.

Teary-eyed, Anna licked her lips, then she said, "Okay. Let's stop at this motel and rent a room." Austin's face glowed with relief. Anna nodded and said, "But, we should... we shouldn't park out in the open. Let's park in-between the buildings. Behind a cactus or something. They won't know where we are if we hide the car and hide in a motel room, right?"

"*Right.*"

Austin tightly gripped the wheel and inhaled deeply as the duo passed the diner. There were a handful of people inside of the eatery, chattering with each other and devouring their food. As the sedan escaped the illumination of the roadside eatery, the photographer took a sharp right. The sedan jounced on the dirt as the vehicle rolled to a stop beside a cactus and behind a dried shrub. With a turn of the key, the sedan was swallowed by the ominous darkness.

Austin said, "Just leave everything here, except your phone. We don't need an extra set of clothes or anything like that. Let's just get the hell out of here."

Austin quietly exited the vehicle, keeping the ruckus to a minimum. He stared at the neighboring motel with narrowed eyes. He examined the strangely ominous building, baffled by the forbidding atmosphere. With Anna by his side, he sauntered towards the structure – abandoning the sedan in the horrifying abyss.

The motel appeared regular on the surface. There were only two floors with a dozen rooms each, and the rooms were easily accessible from the parking lot. There were only four vehicles in the parking lot – a slow night. The main office sat at the foyer of the parking area, below a neon sign. In bold cursive, the crimson sign read: *Gates Motel 15.*

The most peculiar part of the establishment was the structure behind the motel – a large house. Standing three stories high, a palatial home with dingy brick walls resided behind the motel. Several rooms in the stately house were clearly illuminated. Yellow light pierced through the windows. The house seemed perfect for a maniacal person.

As the pair approached the main office, Austin gazed at the towering house and whispered, "Where the hell did we end up?"

***

Austin and Anna peered into the office through the glass door. The room was simple. There were two sofas beside the door and a hardwood desk directly across the entrance. An elderly man stood behind the table, swaying like if he were standing on a rocking boat as he dozed in-and-out of consciousness – practically sleeping with his eyes open. The man was certainly strange, but he seemed harmless. The couple entered the office.

Austin knocked on the desk and said, "Hello. We'd like to rent a room for the night."

The elderly man erratically blinked as if he were awoken from a deep slumber. He said, "Oh, welcome, welcome. My name is Charles. I'm the owner of this... this *fine* establishment. How can I help you tonight, folks?"

Austin furrowed his brow and stepped in reverse as he examined the man. He could handle a pinch of oddness in a person, but he was frightened of escaping one psychopath and landing in the clutches of another. He couldn't easily trust the elder. His trust issues were justified after enduring such a violent day.

Charles stood five-eight with a delicate figure – a gentle breeze could knock him over. He had a small bald spot towards the center of his dome, surrounded by bushy grizzled hair. His blue eyes were indecipherable. His face was covered in gnarled wrinkles. He wore a red sweater, rumpled gray slacks, and brown dress shoes.

Austin said, "We'd like to rent a room. Just one night. We'll be out by morning."

Charles responded, "Okay. We only accept cash at the moment. I'm not into the whole credit and debit scam. I'm a paper man. If I can't feel it, then I don't have it. So, it'll run you about $50 a night. An extra $20 since you don't have a reservation. Sound good?"

Austin nodded and said, "Sure..." He turned towards Anna and asked, "You have $70? Or at least fifty? I think I have a twenty in my wallet."

As the pair organized their finances, Charles sighed and stared at the ceiling. His lips moved as if he were speaking, but he did not utter a sound. He shuddered and nodded, then he continued his inaudible conversation with the ceiling. He burst into a gentle giggle, holding his knobbly hand to his mouth. As she handed her boyfriend a fifty-dollar bill, Anna stared at Charles with a furrowed brow – bewildered.

Austin planted the money on the table and said, "Here you go. Can we have a key?"

Charles blinked erratically as his conversation was disrupted. He sneered in annoyance at Austin, curling his lip and glaring with sharp eyes. The elderly man was clearly busy with his ceiling and the couple did not mind stampeding over his plans. Austin raised his brow as he stared back at the man. He didn't feel threatened. He was, however, confused.

Charles smiled and said, "You've got to fill out a form before you head to your room. Record keeping and such. You know the deal."

"Okay, okay..."

As Austin filled out the standard form, sloppily scribbling across each line, Charles examined his key rack. The selection was wide on account of the slow night – only four of the 24 rooms were occupied. Yet, he had trouble choosing a key. He could have yanked any key from the wall, but he was contemplating his move. Suspicion reigned supreme.

Anna asked, "Can we use your phone?"

Charles tossed a key on the counter – *Room 104.*

He furrowed his brow and asked, "What for?"

"We have to call the cops. We've been running into some trouble lately. Please, can we use your phone? It'll only take a minute."

Charles puckered his lips and nodded. He said, "*No.* But, you can use the phone in your room. No long distance calls, though. Make sure the police are local. I don't want any of that FBI bullshit around here. It's not good for business."

Austin signed his name, then he stared up at Charles. He glanced at Anna and nodded, agreeing with her bemused expression. The man's nonchalant negligence was baffling. Austin simply sighed and grabbed the key. He was not going to argue with the odd man. He had made enough enemies for one night.

As the pair strolled towards the exit, Charles said, "Wait." Austin and Anna turned towards the man, anxious. Charles said, "Don't forget to leave a review before you leave in the morning. You know, one of those internet reviews. It helps us get more business."

Mystified, Austin nodded and said, "Sure..."

Charles sternly said, "I'm serious, boy. Don't forget."

The couple simultaneously nodded and waved at the elderly man – *bye.* The man's constant shifts in mood were frightening and the pair couldn't handle it. They strolled out of the office, then they scampered towards their assigned room.

***

Austin turned the doorknob, then he slowly

shoved the door open. Like a tsunami, the pearly moonlight poured into the humble motel room. Particles of dust danced through the air in front of the door, swaying with the sudden opening. A foul stench, like a body decomposing during a blazing summer, hurtled towards the door – the miasma itself was trying to escape the small chamber.

Pinching his nose, Austin stepped into the room and said, "It's better than dying out there, I guess..."

Anna pressed her nose on Austin's shirt, relishing in the aroma of his sweet cologne. She whispered, "Anything's better than dying out there."

Austin shut the door behind him, then he glanced around the room. There was a window to the right of the door; the filthy glass barrier was veiled by cracked blinds and dusty black curtains. Next to the window, there was a small round table with a single chair. The rest of the room was obscured by the lingering shadows.

The photographer strolled forward, then he stopped at a nightstand. With the turn of a knob, the lamp illuminated the dingy room. The chamber was rather simple. There was a queen-sized bed beside the nightstand; the sheets were wrinkled, but the stains were kept to a minimum. Across from the foot of the bed, there was a dresser with a tube television on top. There was also a bathroom at the other end of the room.

Austin said, "Go ahead and freshen up if you want."

Anna trudged towards the bathroom and said, "Yeah, sure."

The bed squealed as Austin sat down beside the nightstand. There was a landline phone and a thick bible beside the lamp. Austin held the landline phone to his ear and tapped the keys, but to no avail. The phone was out of service. He checked his cellphone and found the same unfortunate results – no reception.

Austin whispered, "Why wouldn't he let us use his phone?"

Anna stood at the doorway as she glanced around the small bathroom. There was a sink and a toilet to the left, a bathtub-shower combination directly ahead, and a window to the right. The window led to the back of the building. The bathroom was simple and efficient, but the grime was undeniable. The young woman shook her head, disgusted by the lack of hygiene. She returned to Austin's side.

As he despondently gazed at his phone, Austin asked, "You mind trying out your cellphone?"

Anna asked, "Why? What's wrong?"

"The old man lied. The phone doesn't work. I don't have signal on my phone, either. Check yours."

Anna bit her bottom lip and gently shuddered. The anxiety began to build up in her body, returning with full force. She checked her phone, then she whimpered. She had no reception in the dismal room. Holding the phone over her head ended with the same result. She thought she escaped the dead zone, but she simply descended deeper into the madness.

Austin gently rubbed her shoulder and said in a soft tone, "Calm down, sweetheart. Everything's going to be okay. We're going to get out of this, remember? Nothing's going to happen to us. I won't let them touch a hair on your head."

Austin planted a soft kiss on Anna's forehead. He walked towards the door, then he peered through the peephole – the parking lot was silent and vacant. He checked each lock on the door twice, ensuring their maximum protection. He moved the rickety chair in the room, jamming the piece of furniture under the doorknob.

Austin whispered, "Everything's going to be okay..."

Austin and Anna sank into the rough mattress. The rugged mattress was more like a pile of rocks than a fluffy cloud, but the couple could manage. The filth did not bother them. Their minds were already polluted by the horrendous sight of murder. Dread was difficult to ease. It clung to minds like a needy child clinging to his mother – the grip was mighty. The couple found themselves reflecting on the unfortunate trip. Austin thought about his photo-shoot and the health of his career; Anna pondered the potential differences in the trip if she never joined.

Breaking the silence, Anna said, "I'm sorry for jumping into your trip at the last minute. You probably would have been an hour ahead of schedule if it wasn't for me."

Austin said, "Don't talk like that. It's not your fault. We can sit here and blame ourselves all day, but it's not our fault. We didn't hurt anyone, we didn't do anything wrong." He gently ran his fingertips across Anna's throat, reassuring her with his soft touch. He said, "Besides, I would never admit it on any other day, but I sort of like it when you tag along."

Anna smirked and said, "I know you do. Thank you..." She nuzzled his neck, seeking comfort in her boyfriend's embrace. With a tear streaming down her cheek, the young woman said, "It's just so scary. I'm afraid we're not going to... It's hard to even say it. I'm afraid we might not 'make it,' I guess."

Austin caressed his girlfriend's hair and said, "We're going to be fine, Anna. I promise, we're going to get through this. A cop is dead. He was killed by those monsters and there's no denying that. They can close a gas station, they can move a station wagon, and they can hide bodies, but they *can't* hide a cop's murder. They can't... I promise, we're going to *make it.*"

The assessment seemed rational, but it did not matter. Time was the most significant element in the game – time was power. If the vicious brothers found the couple first, an army of police officers searching the interstate in the early morning did not matter. Each party was racing against time, watching the timer countdown to zero. Anna buried her face in Austin's chest, whimpering as she tried to sleep.

Chapter Eleven

The Loud Neighbors

The wall behind the headrest trembled with a booming *bang* sound. The fragile wall ghoulishly groaned from the powerful impact in the neighboring room, like if the delicate barrier were jabbed by a heavyweight boxer. The ghastly groan echoed through the room – a cry for help from an inanimate object.

Austin and Anna sat up in bed, awakened by the racket. Austin glanced at the window. Moonlight seeped through the curtains. Morning had not yet arrived. He stared back at the wall with wide eyes. Anna crawled towards the foot of the bed, perturbed by the worrisome ruckus. She feared the wall as much as she feared the noise, like if the wall would collapse on the couple.

Anna asked, "You heard that, right? What was it?"

As he gazed at the wall, Austin responded, "It's... It's probably nothing. Maybe someone's moving some furniture or maybe there's a little fight going on. I don't know."

Austin and Anna stumbled off the bed as another bang reverberated through their simple room. The wall vibrated from the violent blow, creaking from the impact. The pair staggered towards the dresser, their eyes locked on the weak barrier. Huddled together like penguins in a snowstorm, the pair anxiously waited for the next bang – waiting for a person to tear through the wall. Yet, only silence followed the strange attacks.

Anna bit her bottom lip, frightened. She asked, "What the hell is going on over there, Austin? What are they doing? Shit, what if–"

Austin held his index finger up – *quiet.* He whispered, "I'm going to listen, okay? Wait here."

"Wait, wait. Don't be stupid..."

Disregarding his girlfriend's pleas, Austin crept towards the wall, walking on his tiptoes with his shoulders stiff and high. He planted his ear on the wall and protruded his bottom lip, listening to the neighboring racket. *Walls as thin as paper,* he thought, *probably as weak as paper, too.* He couldn't help but feel vulnerable next to the wall.

From the dresser, Anna asked, "Do you hear anything?"

Shh! – Austin loudly shushed Anna. Being rude was not on his mind, he needed absolute silence to hear the other side. Anna understood the fact very well. She held her hands to her mouth and stared at her boyfriend. The wall was horrifying, her thoughts were appalling, but her boyfriend offered some comfort.

Austin furrowed his brow as he listened. He could hear indistinct muttering emerging from the other room, a conversation of bickering and quarreling. There was a tender female voice and a smooth male voice. A simple argument was a possibility – nothing out of the ordinary. Domestic abuse was nothing to scoff at, but survival seemed likely under the circumstances.

Before he could depart the frigid wall, Austin heard a hoarse male voice. The third voice was sonorous and indistinct, a ghastly mumble. With the additional voice, the setting became ominous. Danger lurked around the corner. He could not identify anyone in the other room. He tried to remember Dante's voice and accent, but the attempt was hopeless. The previous afternoon felt like it occurred a week ago.

Austin whispered, "Dante? Clyde?"

Austin hopped and gasped as the wall violently trembled from another thud. He lurched towards Anna, never taking his eyes off the wall. The bang was followed by a woman's shrill shriek. The cry of agony seeped into the room, tormenting the helpless couple. Once again, the disturbing ruckus stopped in an instant.

As her bottom lip quivered, Anna asked, "Are they... Are they killing someone else? Austin, are they killing someone in the other room?"

Perplexed, Austin stared at the wall and answered, "I don't know."

"They're killing someone, aren't they? They're torturing us by killing someone else. They're... They're trying to lure us out of the room. It's Dante and his brother, isn't it? *Isn't it?*"

Austin could not conjure a better response. He repeated, "I don't know."

Anna placed her palm on her moist forehead as she sniffled and shuddered. Her nose was pink from the constant weeping. She couldn't help herself. She was a horror movie lover with a wild imagination. For the simple trip, her twisted imagination blended with reality. The nightmares she adored had transcended fiction.

Anna glanced at Austin and asked, "Should we go over to the other room to try to help?" Austin did not respond. Anna sniffled, then she said, "They're hurting her. I know she's not acting, she's not with them. *They're hurting her.* I know if it were me over there, I'd want someone to help. I'd be praying for anyone to burst through that door and help. But... I don't know. I can't... I can't even think straight anymore!"

Austin agreed with Anna. He would want help in the victim's position and he wanted to provide some assistance. Fear was debilitating, fear crippled him. He searched the room for a viable weapon, but to no avail. Dante was stabbed in the stomach and it did not stop him. A lamp wouldn't do much harm.

Austin wrapped his arms around Anna. He said, "I wish we could help, but we can't. We're no use to anyone right now. If we leave this room, we'd just be walking into trouble, especially if we try to help. When they get tired, we can go to the clerk and ask for help or... or we can run to the car. We can't try to fight them, though. I can't do that. I'm sorry, Anna. I'm sorry for being weak, for being–"

Anna held her index finger to Austin's lips and rapidly shook her head. She said, "No, no, no. I understand. I shouldn't have brought it up. It's not your fault. We... We can't save everyone."

Austin nervously chuckled and wiped a tear from

his eye. He said, "We haven't saved *anyone,* Anna. Not the couple in the station wagon, the gas station cashier, the cop, this woman next door... We're bringing death everywhere we go."

Harbingers of death, Anna thought. She didn't dare utter the idea. The melancholy was strong enough already, she didn't want to add fuel to the flames. The couple were guilt-ridden. Their decision was not made without great regret. Anna buried her face in Austin's chest; Austin nuzzled Anna's hair. The waiting game was set in motion.

***

Austin and Anna slinked towards the grimy bed. The bed squealed with the slightest movement, a shrill howl. Yet, the couple sought comfort. The pair wanted to block the ruckus emerging from the neighboring room by moving along in a regular fashion. Guilt loomed around the corner, teasing the cowardly duo, but they understood the risk would be fruitless.

As the pair cuddled in bed, the couple were interrupted by the sound of a door opening. The hinges grated, echoing through the parking lot and through every vacant room – the dilapidated motel was in dire need of maintenance. Thudding footsteps followed, more than one pair. Austin and Anna gazed at the blank ceiling, enfeebled by fear.

Anna whispered, "Are... Are they leaving?"

Austin did not respond. Without taking his eyes off the ceiling, he squinted and tilted his head, like if he were looking at an interesting artifact in a museum. He was mulling a decision to run, regardless of the consequential ruckus. The neighboring door was opened and people surely walked out, but the noise came to an abrupt end before he could decide.

Anna tapped Austin's sturdy chest and whispered, "What do we do? Huh? What are they doing?" She sobbed and wheezed – an outburst of uncontrollable emotions. She stuttered, "Wh–Why are they doing this to us? *Why?*"

Snapping out of his contemplation, Austin sat up and said, "Let's go. Let's get the hell out of here. We'll make a run for the car or at least the manager's office. Let's get the hell out of here. Come on."

"Let me grab my phone..."

As Austin stood from the bed, the entire window shattered. The window exploded into dozens of sharp shards as a body was thrown through the glass. The body's momentum was reduced by the rustling blinds and dusty curtains, but the window treatments could not withstand the force. Veiled by the detached curtains, the body rolled towards the center of the room.

Austin and Anna stumbled back towards the bathroom, awed by the shocking intrusion. The couple stared at the nude body – a woman. The petite, raven-haired woman twitched on the ground, tangled in the curtains and snapped blinds. She twitched like a drug addict searching for another hit. She was covered in grisly lacerations, each cut dripping blood like leaking faucets.

Austin staggered towards the battered woman.

He said, "Miss... Are you..." He stopped and shook his head before asking the redundant question – of course she wasn't okay. Austin glanced at Anna and said, "Get in the bathroom. Hide or run."

Anna shook her head and said, "No. Let's go together, let's–"

A maniacal chuckle reverberated through the room, fiendish and derisive. Dante stepped towards the broken window with his arms extended from his body, like if he were welcoming a hug. He had a smug smile plastered on his face. His checkered shirt and jeans were still doused in blood. He didn't bother to change during his killing spree. He wore the blood with pride.

Dante protruded his head into the room and glanced at the door. He smirked upon spotting the reinforced lock and the chair – noble but futile attempts. He couldn't help but laugh as he glanced back at the frightened couple. He was gratified to finally reunite with his road trip friends. The gasoline station incident seemed like so long ago.

Dante said, "I told you they'd try to lock the door. They're not too kind to people like us, but I told you that woman would make a great battering ram. I told you so, Clyde, I told you so."

On cue, Clyde stepped towards the broken window. Clyde, a 'thing' of urban legend, stood beside his brother – a few inches taller and a hundred pounds heavier. The brawny man wore a filthy Henley shirt. The white shirt became beige from the grime and age. The garment was covered by a bloodied white apron. He wore loose, tattered

black trousers. He had the appearance of a butcher –
a killer of men and women.

Yet, the couple were more frightened of the man's
physical appearance than his clothing. Clyde had a
head of long black hair protruding every which way.
The wild hair covered some of his inconsistent bald
patches. He had several large lumps on his forehead
and beneath his unkempt hair. The protruding lump
on the right side of his head caused his eye to droop.
His skin was yellow and coarse, discolored and
rugged.

Austin and Anna were aghast by his appearance.
Although certainly disrespectful under any other
circumstance, they couldn't help themselves. They
were shamelessly terrified by his disfigurements.
Austin clenched his jaw and glanced at the
bathroom – he could see the window.

He shoved Anna into the small room and shouted,
"Run and get help!"

Surprised by the butchers' violent entrance and
Austin's push, Anna tumbled into the bathroom. She
fell on her buttocks beside the bathtub. Before she
could utter a word, Austin closed the door. He pulled
all of his weight away from the door, ensuring his
persistent girlfriend could not escape the bathroom.
His actions were valiant and foolish – a sacrifice for
the woman he loved.

Anna tugged on the door knob and shouted,
"Don't do this! Don't leave me!"

Austin yelled, "Lock the door! Lock the damn
door and run, Anna!"

Anna banged on the door and shouted, "No! No,

damn it!"

"The longer you wait, the faster they'll kill me! Run! Run, so... so I can fight back."

Anna stopped pummeling the door and staggered back. She wept into her hands, knowing her tantrum was limiting Austin's opportunities to survive. Kicking and screaming or punching and wailing, her actions could not stop her boyfriend. He would die trying to keep the door closed. As the trembling door settled and the lock's *click* emerged, Austin glanced back at the brothers. He rushed towards the bed, slipping and sliding with each step.

From the broken window, Dante mockingly said, "Run, run. Get help." He childishly giggled and shook his head. He asked, "You think we'd just be standing here if she could escape? It's impossible. Don't be so foolish, boy."

Dante and Clyde climbed through the broken window. Dante lunged over the barrier, keeping his hands away from the glass. Clyde, on the other hand, did not mind the glass piercing into his coarse palms as he climbed over. He didn't feel the same pain as his brother. Clyde hobbled as he pulled a meat tenderizer mallet from the back of his waistband. Dante simpered as he ran towards the back of the room.

Austin yanked the lamp off the nightstand. He glanced at Dante, then towards Clyde. Although Dante was rushing towards the bathroom, Clyde seemed to be the greater threat. Austin gritted his teeth and swung the metal lamp at Clyde. The metal vibrated as it collided with Clyde's thick dome, but the butcher was not affected.

Austin staggered in reverse and whispered, "What the hell?"

The sound of a door knob rattling echoed through the room – a worrisome sound. Austin's eyes widened as he spotted Dante trying to break into the bathroom, pushing and kicking at the door. The conniving hitchhiker used his gargantuan brother as a distraction. He was certain Austin couldn't stop Clyde.

Austin shouted, "Anna, run! He's coming!" The photographer scrambled across the mattress and yelled, "Run!"

Clyde rushed forward, each step causing the floor to tremble. He grabbed the back of Austin's shirt and pulled him back. Austin lost his footing from the butcher's sheer force. Clyde lifted the mallet over his head, then he struck down at the back of Austin's dome. Austin plummeted to the floor from the vicious strike. His leg violently trembled and his body shuddered uncontrollably.

As Clyde lifted the mallet over his head for one final blow, Dante said, "Wait a second, boy. We don't want him dead. Daddy wants him to join us for dinner. Come over here and help me open this damn door. She's got us locked out."

Anna whimpered in the bathroom as she tugged on the window to no avail. She could hear the conversation in the other room, she could hear Austin's unfortunate defeat. The voices were muffled, but the grappling and shouting were distinct. Despite her strongest efforts, exerting all of the energy she could muster, the window wouldn't budge. It was sealed prior to their visit.

Tears gushed from her eyes as she muttered, "Damn it... Damn it..."

Anna hopped and gasped as the door trembled and groaned from a brutish attack – *Clyde*. She sobbed as she stared at her reflection on the begrimed window. Her options were exhausted. She clenched her jaw and stepped back, then she thrust her bare elbow through the window. The glass shattered into a dozen shards, slicing through her tender arm. The sound of wood cracking followed the shattering glass as the door was kicked open. Anna hit the glass again, breaking the remaining shards with her elbow.

Before she could climb out, Clyde grabbed her waist and yanked her out of the bathroom. The giant man tossed the petite woman on the bed like a doll. Dante jumped on Anna, pouncing like a predator on his prey. Zany-eyed, he laughed as he jabbed at Anna's face, striking down at her with all of his might. Each punch dazed the woman until she was knocked unconscious. Blood erupted from her mouth as she coughed and grunted.

Mounted on top of the young woman, Dante smiled and said, "I think that will do it. Let's start packing."

***

Clyde tossed Austin's unconscious body on the bed beside Anna and the black-haired woman. The other victim barely clung to consciousness, dazed and bemused. Her diminutive awareness did not bother the brothers. The trio of victims were bruised and covered in blood, some more than others.

As he stared at the group, Dante licked his lips, then he said, "We have a great selection tonight. A great selection, indeed." He furrowed his brow and turned towards his brother. He asked, "What time is it anyway? It must be early morning by now. I'm starved. I missed dinner because of these two."

Clyde hunched over and held his hands to his chin, shrugging and curling his fingers. He indistinctly muttered, uttering the sound of a few letters. He couldn't complete a word, let alone a sentence. Dante knew his brother was incapable of speaking, but he spoke to him like any other person. The man was demented, but he wanted his brother to feel like part of the group – he wanted him to feel normal.

Dante said, "Yeah, we can call it a late dinner or an early breakfast. Whatever you like..."

"What the *hell* happened here?! You goddamn bastards destroyed the place! How the hell am I going to fix all of this crap, goddammit?!" Charles shouted from the broken window. "Who the hell do you think you are?!"

Clyde shook his head and retreated to a corner – an oafish man afraid of a delicate elder. He indistinctly muttered and pointed at the trio of guests on the bed – *them, them, them.* Dante nodded as he pointed at the beaten group, following his brother's lead. Pointing the blame at someone else was always easier than taking responsibility.

Dante said, "It was them, daddy. We've been chasing them around for hours. They've been causing nothing but trouble."

Enraged, Charles stomped and yelled, "I don't give a damn, you stupid fuck! You idiots ruined this damn room! And they paid cash, motherfucker, they deserved to be treated better than this!" He frowned and lifted his arms, angry and disappointed. He said, "Look, you got blood on the damn bed sheets and curtains. I just cleaned those last month, boy. You know I hate laundry... I hate doing the damn laundry!"

"I'm sorry, daddy. We were just getting ready to go."

"Then, go on! Get out of here! Take the meat to the house and don't you dare start dinner until I get back. I'll stay here and start cleaning up. I'll fake some accident or something. Maybe an earthquake or a small tornado... I don't know, I'll tell those pigs something if they show up."

Dante nodded, agreeing with his eccentric father. He gently tapped Clyde's shoulder, then he pointed at the bodies. Clyde grunted and moaned as he grabbed the two women – he tossed Anna over his shoulder and held the other woman in his arm like a shopping bag. Dante clenched his jaw as he dragged Austin out of the room.

Watching his children abscond from the obliterated room, Charles shook his head and said, "You damn kids... You goddamn kids..."

Chapter Twelve

The Madhouse

Austin gasped, grasping for air with a raspy inhale. Sweat poured out of his glands like roaring rivers, drenching his body. A strand of his hair dangled towards his nose, dripping from the moisture. The room's searing heat and the anxiety were responsible for his sweat – he was practically melting. He blinked erratically as he glanced around the room.

Austin's wrists and ankles were restrained to the wall by thick metal shackles. He stood on his knees, but he could not stagger to his feet or reach for his pockets. The clanking chains were installed on the dingy brick wall behind him. The walls were spattered with blood, like if they had served as canvases for splatter paintings.

Slits of light pierced through the dusty floorboards above, illuminating the dungeon and penetrating the lingering musk. S-shaped meat hooks dangled from the ceiling and support beams, swaying with the most negligible draft. The concrete floor was mopped with blood. The pungent scent of bleach arose from the cracked ground.

Austin rapidly blinked, trying to clear his blurred vision. Across the room, he could see a woman chained to the parallel wall. Her head was slumped downward and her face was covered by her black hair. The woman was nude and covered in grisly lacerations, like if she had crawled through a field of shattered glass – or like if she were thrown through a window. Despite the lack of formal introductions, he recognized the woman from the motel.

Austin coughed, clearing his throat, then he whispered, "Hey... Hey, are you awake? Are you okay?" The woman did not respond. Austin leaned forward, but he was yanked back by the chains. He whispered, "Miss... Hey, are you awake? Do you know where we are? Please, wake up. Talk to me... Tell me you're alive, tell me you're okay... Tell me I'm not alone."

The young woman was breathing, but she did not awaken. In her involuntary slumber, she did not hear the photographer's soft whisper. The gentle words did not rejuvenate her tormented soul. Words could not heal her physical pain. She was clinging to life, but she was already dead. She had lost all hope.

Austin turned to his right. The sound of munching emerged – an animal feasting on a meal, slurping and burping. The irritating noise, like a swarm of flies buzzing by busy ears, was consistent. A large silhouette was hunched over an unknown object in the corner. Austin was not dim, he knew who was in the corner – *Clyde*.

Austin leaned forward and squinted for a better view. Miraculously, the squint worked – or perhaps his eyes simply adjusted to the darkness. He could see the large man sitting in the corner. His motions were eerie, feral and peculiar, but the environment was much more terrifying. There was a sea of mutilated bodies beside Clyde.

Severed limbs, decapitated heads, and gooey organs were sprawled across the floor like chew toys for an undomesticated dog. There were two decapitated females pinned onto the wall like nudie posters in a teenager's room. The woman on the right was skinned, leaving her tender flesh vulnerable to the world. Although he was certain Anna was not pinned to the wall – she was far more petite than the two victims – the sight made him bawl.

Clyde turned towards Austin's weeping, then he screamed at the top of his lungs. The blurt was indistinct, but his rage and confusion were evident. The hulking man was disoriented by Austin's crying. He staggered to his feet, then he wagged a dismembered human arm at the photographer. He could only mimic his father's scolding actions.

Saliva dripping from his mouth and tears streaming down his cheeks, Austin shouted, "Oh, God! No! No!"

Austin wheezed as he looked away. The arm had deep bite marks and missing flesh. Clyde's lips and chin were drenched in blood. Linking the pieces together was not difficult – *cannibalism.* Clyde walked towards Austin, shaking the mutilated limb at the captive like if he were offering a bite. Austin's refusal was insulting.

Clyde groaned and moaned, muttering like a child with a deep raspy voice. His words were indecipherable, like a baby's vocabulary. Clyde threw the arm on the ground, frustrated and offended, then he marched back to his side of the room. He riffled through a desk, searching for a weapon – knives, screwdrivers, saws, hammers and the like filled the arsenal.

Austin stared at the breathing woman and shouted, "Wake up! Wake up, damn it! Wake up!" He glanced back at Clyde and gasped. He shouted, "Oh, shit! *Shit!*"

Clyde hurtled towards the captive with a hammer. He swung the hammer with all of his might, missing by an inch. Austin jerked away, weaving and bobbing his head like an audience member searching for a better view of the stage. He was quick and nimble, even with the restraints. Clyde grunted, then he swung again. The hammer vibrated as the tool clashed with the wall.

Austin said, "Wait, wait, wait. Please, listen to me. We weren't trying to hurt you. We're good people, Clyde." Clyde tilted his head and lowered the hammer upon hearing his name. Austin sniffled and nodded, then he said, "Yeah, I know your name. I know you, Clyde. I just... I just want to help you. That's all. We don't want to hurt you or your family. We want to help you get better. Please, don't do this. Just let us go."

Clyde stepped in reverse and gazed into Austin's eyes. He did not understand the words, other than his name, but he could read the man's aura. The photographer was harmless. Austin stared back at Clyde, trying his best to keep his poker face afloat. He was revolted by Clyde's appearance and the surrounding gore, but he kept his eyes sharp and sincere.

Clyde slowly shook his head and stammered, "N–N–N–N–No..."

Austin glanced up at the ceiling and yelled, "Help! Help! Damn it! Help us!"

Clyde rushed forward, then he swung the hammer. The hammer hit Austin's right shoulder. Austin grimaced from the pain as he tugged away. Clyde struck down again, slicing through the air with his mighty swing.

As the pair grappled in a one-sided fight, the young woman awoke. Teary-eyed, she stared at the duo in utter disbelief. Her tender dreams ended and she was tossed back into a restless nightmare. She felt sympathy for Austin. At the same time, she couldn't help but loathe him for waking her up.

The woman yelled, "Help! Help!"

Clyde turned towards the woman and muttered. He held his hands to his ears and shouted. Frustrated by the ruckus, he tugged on his hair and stomped on the ground. Like a spoiled child at a toy store, he threw tantrums quite often – it was part of his childish demeanor. He turned back towards Austin, then he swung the hammer again. Austin was set free as the hammer struck the dilapidated chain restraining his left arm.

With one wide eye, Clyde bellowed. He slapped the thick lumps on his forehead, punishing himself for his foolish mistake. The slaps did not physically harm him, but each hit prepared him for pain. He knew his father would beat him without mercy for his recklessness. He would be brutally punished for

118

his actions.

Seizing the opportunity, Austin struck Clyde's groin with a powerful uppercut. Fortunately, the huge man's genitals were as sensitive as those on any other person. There may have been another lump or two down there, but the coarse and rugged skin could not stop the agony. Clyde staggered in reverse. He stumbled over the severed arm he was eating, then he plummeted to the ground. A loud thud reverberated through the room as the back of his head collided with the concrete. The ground trembled from the fall.

Austin leaned forward, peering at the menacing man. He expected him to sit up in one swift movement, like every serial killer in his favorite horror movies. The woman on the parallel wall followed his lead, staring at the man with hopeful eyes. With vengeance on her mind, she wanted her captor to suffer an agonizing death. To her dismay, Clyde was only knocked unconscious by the blow to his head.

***

Austin cried as he reached for the hammer to no avail. Every inch aggravated his injured shoulder. He could not endure the stinging pain. He leaned back on the wall and sobbed. His attempts were fruitless – all of them. He couldn't escape the butcher brothers, he couldn't fight off Clyde in the motel room, and he could not save his girlfriend. He was a coward in dull, worn-out armor.

From across the room, the woman said, "Don't stop now. Don't you dare stop now. They'll kill us if we don't escape. Keep trying. Break us free."

With a grimace, Austin said, "I can't... I can't do it..."

"*You have to.* Please, don't let them win like this. Don't let them kill us. You have one free arm, you have the chance to save us. Come on, try something. You can do this."

Austin stared down at the hammer and shook his head. A motivational speech could not shorten the distance between a man and a tool. If he were to survive, he would need both functioning arms. Amplifying the pain on his shoulder would do the pair no good in the long run. Instead, he glanced at the arsenal of tools to his right.

He could not reach the hammer, so surely he could not reach Clyde's arsenal. However, the makeshift tools spilling towards him like a wave at shore were useful – severed limbs, decapitated heads, and bones. A mountain of bones, the Mount Everest of death, provided the tools necessary for escape.

The woman glanced at the bones and said, "Yeah, yeah... *Do it.* You can break the chains, then break mine. Please, hurry."

Austin shut his eyes and blindly grabbed a random bone. He opened his eyes to a squint to briefly examine his choice. He found himself with a sturdy humerus – an arm bone. It was not nearly as reliable as a hammer, but he would have to make-do. He didn't want to think about the situation, either. Using the bones of a slain person for his escape made him queasy.

As Austin struck the restraint on his right arm, the woman nervously smiled and said, "You can do it. Thank you. Thank you so much." Overwhelmed with joy, she cried and moaned. As she recomposed herself, the woman said, "My... My name is Helen. Please, remember that in case anything happens to me. My name is Helen... Thank you."

In the same fashion as Helen, Austin cried – the joy was contagious. He destroyed the restraints on his legs. He could not break the shackles from his ankles, so he broke the wall mounts instead. He would rather drag the chains with him than die in the disgusting dungeon. His legs wavered as he staggered to his feet.

Patting the blood and dust from his pants, Austin said, "It's nice to meet you, Helen. My name is Austin."

Helen nodded and said, "Okay, okay. I think we should wait to talk. We don't have too much time for introductions. Please, break these damn chains so we can leave. Hurry."

Austin nodded in agreement. Yet, he could not rush to Helen's aid. He tiptoed over Clyde's unconscious body, examining every nook and cranny on his disfigured face. He could not overcome his fears. He expected Clyde to spring upward like a Jack-in-the-box toy – the melody even rang through his head, teasing him.

The floorboards above moaned like the undead in a horror movie – slow, ghastly groans. A woman's soft whisper and a man's frustrated mutter could be heard from the basement. The conversation was indistinct, cluttered words and letters. Although he could not clearly identify the voices, he had a decent idea.

Austin whispered, "Anna..."

Helen sternly said, "Austin, *help me.* Please, stop wasting time. Break these damn shackles and let's get the hell out of here. *Please.*"

Austin picked up the hammer and said, "I'll help you break free, but I'm not leaving this place without my girlfriend. And, if they touched a single hair on her body, I'm not going to leave until I slaughter all of these bastards."

Helen gazed at her savior with inquisitive eyes, awed by the love he shared with his girlfriend. She said, "That's... That's fine. I'll get help. I'll bring the cops to this place. I swear, I'll help you as much as possible. I promise."

Austin clenched his jaw and struck the chain. The chain clinked and clanked, but it would not break. One, two, or three strikes, it did not matter. The attacks barely scuffed the metal. His restraints were clearly weaker than Helen's chains – or, bone was stronger than metal and he did not realize it.

Wide-eyed, Austin turned towards the staircase to his left. He held his index finger to his lips, shushing Helen – a precautionary measure considering she wasn't speaking in the first place. The basement door slowly opened, the hinges squealing like a pig in mud.

From the top of the stairs, Dante said, "Clyde, how are you doing, buddy? You okay down there?" Clyde did not respond on account of his beating. Dante said, "Listen, pal, I know daddy can be harsh, but it's only because he loves us so much. He doesn't want us to mess everything up. Business was just getting good and we wrecked a room. We should have known better. You understand? Clyde?"

As the first stair groaned, Helen glared at Clyde and shouted, "Kill him! Kill that monster!"

Better to kill one now, Austin thought, *and finish the rest off later.* He rushed forward, then he clobbered Clyde's dome with the hammer. He grunted and wheezed with each strike. Clyde's legs trembled as he received the blows. Austin counted each and every hit, savoring the vengeance – one, two, three, four.

Dante pushed Austin away from his beaten brother. Austin staggered back towards a fragile pillar, confused. In his fit of rage, he did not hear Dante rushing down the stairs. He was temporarily deafened by his lust for vengeance. Before he could even get a glimpse of Dante, Austin faced a sturdy rolling pin.

The rolling pin crushed his nose and dazed him with a single strike. He fell to the floor, overwhelmed by the pain and Helen's shrill cries. He felt numb and baffled, lost in madness. He could barely hear and his vision began to fade. He feared death was approaching, coming for his tormented soul.

Austin narrowed his eyes as he stared at Dante. Dante seemed to be wearing a floral-pattern apron over his bloodied clothing – a peculiar choice for such a savage man. *An ironic display of lunacy,* Austin thought, *or the clothing of a victim? Perhaps a mother killed while baking a pie for her child? A young child... a motherless child.* He did not want to contemplate the sadistic possibilities any further.

Dante gently slapped Clyde's cheek and said, "Wake up, Clyde. Come on, I know you can hear me. I know your thick head is stronger than that. I've got to get ready for dinner. Wake up, boy, I've got to get dressed. I don't have time for this."

Clyde coughed as he awoke. He loudly moaned as he squirmed on the floor, flailing his limbs and screaming. Dante attentively stared at him, soothing his brother's pain with a soft hum. The vicious hitchhiker had a maternal aura, but only when it came to his brother. He was apathetic to the world, slaughtering without mercy, but he cared deeply for his sibling. The love was mutual.

In a soft tone, Dante said, "There you go, buddy. Everything's going to be okay. It's just a little boo-boo. We'll patch you up before dinner, then you can have all you can eat. We have plenty of food to go around tonight, Clyde."

Dante stood and retrieved a chef's knife from the back of his waistband. He walked towards Helen with a smug smile plastered on his face. Helen stared up at the ceiling and screamed. She hollered for help, but there was no response – the floorboards didn't even groan. Dante grabbed the nape of her neck and pulled her closer, leering at her like a pervert at a shopping mall.

He said, "Oh, girl, I wanted to make this easy for the both of us. You should have stayed asleep."

Teary-eyed, Helen scowled and said, "Fuck you

and your fucking brother. You can go fuck each other for all I care, you sick bastards."

"Girl, girl, girl. I'm certainly not going to make it easy for you now."

Dante grabbed a fistful of hair, then he yanked Helen's head back. He sliced into her scalp with the honed blade, cutting through her skin like if he were slicing through warm butter. Back-and-forth, he slowly scalped the woman. Helen shrieked as blood spilled out of the wound, cascading over her face like rainfall on a windshield. The sound of skin being torn, like paper being ripped in an empty auditorium, was as loud as Helen's shrill shriek.

Austin weakly reached for the pair and whispered, "Please, stop... Don't do this... Please..."

Helen gasped as Dante tore her scalp from her dome. Scalp in hand, Dante turned towards Austin. He chuckled at his futile attempt at rescuing the woman. The photographer could barely conjure the energy to speak, he surely couldn't overpower two vicious men. Dante kicked Austin's hand away. He grabbed his rolling pin, then he struck down at Austin's face. The hit instantly knocked him unconscious.

Chapter Thirteen

The Family Dinner

Austin erratically blinked as he awoke, his head slumped down to his chest. His nose was fractured and stained with blood. The dried blood was smeared across his cheeks, lips, and chin. He tried to lift his arms and kick his feet, but he found himself tied to a chair with durable rope.

Austin whispered, "What the... What is this? What the hell is this?" He stared at his body in disbelief. He shouted, "What the hell is this?! What did you do?! You sick pieces of shit, what the hell did you do?"

Austin was restrained to a makeshift chair – a homemade novelty. The sturdy piece of furniture was constructed with human remains – *bones*. The armrests were made of arm bones, the legs were crafted with the finest leg bones, and the seat was comprised of several scapula bones. Austin glanced over his shoulder, examining the rest of the demented seat. The back rails were made up of rib bones, prodding at his spine. He was sitting on a collection of human remains. Several victims were killed for his 'comfort.'

Austin sobbed and said, "Holy shit... You're crazy. You're all crazy." He gritted his teeth and tried to lift his arms, but to no avail. He whispered, "This can't be happening. It can't be real."

Upon hearing a squealing sound above, Austin glanced at the ceiling. He shuddered as he struggled to speak, rendered speechless by fear. Tied from her wrists and ankles, Helen dangled from the ceiling. Covered in lacerations and drenched in blood, she swung above the table like a human chandelier. Blood dripped from her bloody scalp, plopping on the tabletop. The act was inhuman.

As his bottom lip quivered, Austin whispered, "Helen... Helen..."

A door at the other end of the room opened. Charles strolled into the room, nonchalantly whistling. The environment did not bother him. He was the decorator, after all. He took a seat at the other end of the large rectangular dining table, sitting directly across from Austin. The pair were separated by twelve seats – six chairs made of bones at each side.

The young photographer was astonished by Charles' mere appearance inside of the nightmarish home. He furrowed his brow and tilted his head as he examined the old man's indifferent demeanor. Although he did not have all of the pieces, he could formulate a decent theory. *A father figure,* he thought, *the hotel manager was in on it.*

Austin glared at Charles and asked, "Where's Anna? Huh? Where's my girlfriend?" On the verge of tears, he nervously chuckled and grunted. He warned, "I swear, if you hurt her, if you even laid *one* finger on her, I'll rip you to pieces and eat you for dinner. I'll kill all of you! I'll wipe your pathetic family off the face of the earth! You hear me?!"

Disregarding the warning, Charles shouted, "Cheryl! Cheryl, you dumb dog, what time is the food going to be ready?! It's almost going to be morning and I have to sleep soon!" He shook his head and muttered, "Goddammit, I don't have all day... I'm the one that has to work in the morning, I'm the one making all the money around here."

From over Austin's shoulder, Cheryl shouted, "I'll be finished in a minute, dear!"

"Well, hurry it up, woman!"

Austin furrowed his brow and tilted his head. Cheryl's voice caught his attention. The voice belonged to a man, a man trying to speak like a woman. The voice was soft and feminine but clearly forced. Such a cliché tone could not be mistaken for a woman. Austin was not one to judge or assume, but he was certain there was a man hiding behind the curtain.

Charles said, "Hey, boy, you should be *honored* to have dinner with us tonight. We usually don't allow your kind to join us at the family table. No, no, that's like tainting the bloodline. Still, my woman seems to like you. There's something about you. Hell, even I'm falling for you."

As Charles chuckled, snorting like a pig, Austin said, "I'm going to kill you. You understand me? I'm going to kill you and both of your sons. I'll slaughter them like the people you slaughtered for... for..." He glanced down at the chair and shuddered. He said, "Like the people you slaughtered for *this*."

Austin winced as a door behind him opened. He was familiar with the following noise, he had heard it from Anna – high heels thudding on hardwood floorboards. Anna was not entering the room, though, and he was not prepared for Cheryl's grand entrance. Nothing could prepare the young photographer for the madness.

Austin gasped upon spotting Cheryl, then he whispered, "You... You just don't stop..."

Dante wore more than one face, he moved with more than one frame – *literally*. Draped over his figure like a common garment, the sinister hitchhiker wore a suit of tanned female skin up to his neck. His face was smeared with globs of makeup and he wore Helen's scalp on his dome. Over his loose-fitted human suit, he wore a blue sundress beneath a floral-pattern apron. He swung his hips as he strutted towards his father, glancing back at Austin with kittenish eyes. Dante was Cheryl and Cheryl was Dante.

In a soft tone, Dante said, "Oh, honey, our meal is almost ready. It's a very late dinner, but I promise it's going to be worth it. I have our Clyde in the kitchen right now preparing a little feast for my big man and our handsome guest."

Charles said, "Well, you should hurry it up. You know I hate missing my meals. Something's always late in this house and it pisses me off. It gets on my damn nerves."

Dante leaned closer to his father and said, "Oh, I'm sorry, darling. I'll make sure it never happens again." He planted a passionate kiss on Charles' forehead as he glanced back at Austin – he wanted their guest to see. Dante said, "I hope that makes it better."

Charles playfully spanked Dante and said, "Okay, okay. Just finish up and bring the food. I'm starved."

As he watched the peculiar interaction, Austin stuttered, "Wha–What the fuck?"

Dante giggled as he walked back to the kitchen with hurried steps. He waved at Austin, wiggling his fingers at the tormented guest. Austin stared at him with a deadpan expression. He didn't know what emotions to convey. He was angry, frightened, humiliated, and disgusted. He did not know if a grimace of disgust would warrant some sort of hate – he was politically correct, even in the darkest crevices of insanity.

Austin turned towards Charles and said, "You're all insane. But... you know that already, don't you? You just don't give a crap because you're so damn insane. Look at yourself, look at your sons. You don't even know who you are and you have the nerve to kill innocent people for *nothing.* What the hell is wrong with you, old man?"

Charles smirked and said, "Wow. I invite you to dinner in my humble home and this is the thanks I get? This is how you repay me for everything I've done for you? Boy, you better learn some manners unless you want to end up like this bitch up here."

Charles laughed as he pointed at Helen. Austin shook his head and sobbed. For a moment, he had forgotten about her presence and her unfortunate demise. He grunted as he tried to free himself from the chair. The chair had a grip on him, though, like if he were sitting on a living person who was trying to hold him down.

Austin glanced at the bay windows to his left and shouted, "Help! Help! He's killing us! Damn it! He's going to kill me!"

His helpless pleas rebounded back to him from the windows. The shouting did not matter anyway. The closest building was the motel and a motel without guests could not hear. Aid was far beyond his grasps. Austin bounced on the seat, trying to break free. He held his breath as he exerted all of his energy, but to no avail.

Dante entered the room and exclaimed, "Dinner is ready!"

Austin shouted, "No! Please, God, no! Not now!"

Clyde limped into the room, balancing an aluminum tray in his right hand and rubbing the back of his head with his left. There were two bowls on top of the tray. The bowls were made with the top of human skulls. The skulls were scratched, a crack here and there, but the food did not seep through.

Before Clyde could reach his father, Charles said, "Wait, boy. Feed our guest first. I bet he's starving to find out what's for dinner." He glared at Austin with deviant eyes and an officious grin. Charles said, "He's eating good tonight..."

***

Clyde grinned as he hobbled towards the opposite end of the table. He dragged his legs with each step – a product of his deformities and the beating he endured. Yet, he was happy to serve. His childlike exuberance glowed beyond his peculiar appearance. At heart, the savage killer was a confused and innocent child – at least, innocent in his mind.

Austin squirmed away on the chair, kicking and screaming like a child dragged to the doctor's office. With the restraints, he could only move his head so far. Tears gushing from his eyes, the young photographer whimpered. From the furniture comprised of human remains to the peculiar family serving him, he was surrounded by chaos.

Austin said, "Please... Please, I'm begging you, just let us go. We won't tell anyone. We just want to go home. *Please.*"

Charles said, "You're not going anywhere until you try my wife's cooking. As jealous as it makes me, she made it especially for you. Shit, boy, you might even like it. It tastes much better than that crap they serve at the diners down the road. Believe me."

Clyde placed the makeshift bowl in front of Austin. The bowl was welling with a dark red liquid and chunks of cooked meat. It could have been a bowl of pozole – a delicious Mexican soup – but that would be too easy. Assuming the worst, flesh of some sort floated in a small pool of blood. Clyde dipped the spoon into the hot soup, fishing for a slab of meat. Austin's bottom lip quivered as he stared at the makeshift eating utensil. The handle of the spoon was made of finger bones glued and tied together.

Austin whispered, "No, no, no... How could you do this to them?"

Standing beside Clyde and eagerly watching, Dante said, "Oh, Clyde, darling, make sure it's nice and cool for him. You don't want to burn that young man's tongue. I think it might be good for something else..."

Astonished, Austin asked, "What the fuck is wrong with all of you?"

Clyde held his hand beneath the spoon. He gently blew on the scorching soup, ensuring the meat would not fly off the spoon. Like a caring parent, he made a crepitating sound by blowing, fluttering his lips like a horse – as if Austin would allow such an abominable load into his mouth if it resembled a plane or train.

Austin bit his bottom lip and tightly shut his eyes, then he turned away. Clyde mumbled as he pushed the spoon towards their guest, but to no avail. Austin refused to spare even a single glance. Confused, the heavyset man turned towards Dante – the motherly-figure in his life.

Dante shrugged and said, "Sorry, sweetie, he doesn't seem to like our food. Such a shame. We spend so much time preparing for this..."

Dante sighed and stared at his feet, saddened. Clyde glowered and groaned, angered by his sibling's disappointment. He turned towards Austin, then he jammed his stocky fingers into his mouth. He pulled Austin's mouth open, using his fingers as a crowbar. Austin gagged as he tasted the filth lingering on the butcher's fingers.

Before Austin could say a word, Clyde shoved the spoon into his mouth. He pushed Austin's chin, forcing him to chew the tender meat. Austin coughed and gagged as he quickly swallowed. Clyde followed with another spoonful of soup. The photographer grimaced as he quickly chewed and swallowed. He feared he would choke if he did not comply.

With a moment to breathe, Austin said, "Please... Stop... Don't do this..."

Clyde grabbed the bowl, then he dumped the soup into Austin's mouth. Austin coughed and gagged as the boiling soup streamed down his throat and burned his chin and neck. Clyde nodded and laughed, proud of his deed. He was able to feed the man, he was able to please his father, and he was able to redeem his mother's cooking. Dante simpered, then he entered the kitchen.

Austin spat and shook his head as he recomposed himself. He gagged and retched, but not due to the taste. To his utter surprise, the soup actually tasted good. The stew was spicy and the meat was succulent. If he were in a restaurant, he would feel inclined to leave a positive review. It bothered him, though. *It could be anything, but it tasted good,* he thought, *what's wrong with me?*

Clyde limped towards his father. He placed a bowl on the table, then he stepped aside. Dante returned from the kitchen with half of a lemon – his father's preference. Charles grinned from ear-to-ear as he rubbed his hands together, ready to feast on his delectable meal. Charles slurped, then gulped – loud and obnoxious.

He said, "This is absolutely delicious, Cheryl. You, too, Clyde. You've really outdone yourselves this time. It's no wonder our guest had to eat so sloppily.

I was going to scold him for his lack of table manners, but, shit, I want to do the same."

Dante blinked in a kittenish manner. He said, "Thank you, darling. You know we do our best to serve you."

"I know, I know. I can get a bit mean at times, but you always pull through. You're a strong woman, Cheryl. I don't know where I'd be without you. I might have been–"

Austin interrupted, "What did you feed me?"

Charles slurped another spoonful of stew. He said, "Well, we served you some soup with *premium* meat. Cooked to perfection, if I may add." He winked at Dante and chuckled. Charles glanced back at Austin and said, "You see, some people like to eat this meat raw. I mean, I've seen them eat it raw and I generally don't accept it. That's for savages. But, I let them live as they want to live. Who am I to interfere, right? It's none of my business. Me? Well, I don't eat it raw. No, I'm not a savage, you know. I'm not like *those* people."

Eyes full of tears, Austin shook his head and asked, "What... What did you feed me? What did I eat? What kind of 'meat' was that? Please, just tell me the truth. Stop fucking around with me. *Answer me.*"

Charles puckered his lips, then he said, "Cheryl, sweetie, bring out the meat of the day. Show him our finest meat."

As he walked out of the room, Dante said, "Okay. Come here, Clyde, give your mommy a hand. I need a real big boy to help me."

***

With few options, Austin sat on the uncanny chair and anxiously waited for the devious pair to return. He glared at Charles from across the long dining table. Charles continued to slurp the stew. He was quick to correct poor manners, but he happily ate with his mouth open – smacking his lips after each loud slurp. He was a hypocrite, but a stern one. He glanced to his left as the door swung open.

Charles smiled and said, "There you are. Our boy was getting a bit nervous over here. Shaking in his boots."

Empty-handed, Dante entered the room and said, "Oh, you know how they get, sweetie. They love to put up a fight until they finally pass away. I wish we'd kill them sooner. It would make everything so much easier."

"No, no, no, darling, that's nonsense. The meat is fresher while they're alive. The blood is still pumping. You don't want to kill them too soon. You're basically putting a damn expiration date on them by doing that."

Dante sighed, then he said, "Okay, okay. I understand. Clyde, bring the bitch in here and show her to our lovely guest."

Austin whispered, "*Bitch?*"

Clyde walked into the room, lugging a bone chair in his hands. Anna was restrained to the seat, bloodied and gagged. The gag wrapped around her mouth seemed to be made of tanned human skin. Her head swayed as she barely clung to consciousness. She had a fresh gash on her forehead

– she put up a fight.

Austin shook his head and said, "No, no, no. Why... What did you do? What did you do to her, you sick bastards? Why?! What did we do to you? What did we..."

Gooey saliva dribbled from Austin's mouth as he hysterically bawled. The image of his injured girlfriend sent him into a tailspin of overwhelming emotions. He was hit with an overpowering feeling of giddiness. He shivered like a man with a severe fever. The chair groaned from his uncontrollable trembling.

Charles said, "Boy, you're asking the wrong questions. *Stupid questions,* as a matter of fact. 'What did we do?' Shit, we did what we always do. You... Well, you aren't like us, so you probably have different 'moral standards' or some bullshit like that. I mean, to be blunt, son, you ate the girl. Not like the way you folks eat them in the movies, either. I mean: *you ate the girl.*"

Over Charles' devious cackle, Austin shouted, "No! No, damn it!"

Clyde set the chair down beside Austin, then he stepped in reverse. Austin gazed into Anna's eyes – she was a hollow vessel, operating without a soul. Her white tank top was ripped below her breasts. There as a long and deep horizontal cut on her stomach. Her limbs were drenched in blood. Chunks of her arms and back were missing.

Austin was shocked by the heinous revelation. The same thought ran a marathon through his fracturing mind: *I ate her. I ate her. I ate her.* Teary-eyed, he gagged and retched. Thick red vomit splattered on his jeans and plopped on the floor. The chunks of flesh streamed down a river of stew and saliva.

With downcast eyes, Dante said, "Now, that wasn't very nice. We worked very hard on that meal. How could you just throw up like that? You didn't even have the courtesy to ask for a bathroom break..." He clicked his tongue and shook his head, disappointed. As his eyes widened, Dante said, "Oh, I know! It's not my cooking, is it? You must not like *that* meat. You want something else. That's it, isn't it? Well, she has plenty of meat on her. Give me a hand, Clyde."

Dante smiled as he approached Austin. He was not disgusted by the vomit – no one in the family was disgusted by the puke. Clyde lugged the chair a few inches towards Austin, tipping the seat forward on its two front legs. Anna sat only a few inches away from her boyfriend.

Dante said, "Let's see what we can grab."

Dante pulled Austin's hand closer to Anna's torso. Clyde, being a helpful young man, shoved the chair another inch forward. Austin grimaced as his fingers were forced into the large laceration on Anna's stomach. Anna gasped, awakened by the stinging pain.

Austin yelled, "No! No! Stop! Please, stop! Don't... Don't do this!" He gazed into Anna's bloodshot eyes. He said, "I'm sorry. I'm so sorry, sweetheart. I love you, Anna. *I love you.*"

Dante giggled as he pulled Austin's fingers out.

He wouldn't allow the young photographer to have all of the fun. He slipped both of his hands into the thick cut, then he pulled his arms in opposite directions. The skin was torn and blood oozed as the laceration became wider. Anna convulsed and hyperventilated as she gazed into Austin's eyes. She fought for air, but she was overwhelmed by agony. She tried to speak, only conjuring a croak of a word. With the anguish, Anna stopped moving and breathing. She suffered a violent death.

With a quivering lip, Austin asked, "Anna? Anna, are you okay?" A single tear streamed down his cheek. He said, "I'm... I'm sorry, sweetheart. I should have kept driving. I shouldn't have... I shouldn't have picked him up! It's all my fault!"

With his fake fingernails, Dante ripped a piece of Anna's intestine from the wound. He giggled as he examined the piece of flesh with inquisitive eyes, like an archaeologist marveling over an ancient artifact. The small slab of human anatomy was considered a delicacy in the household. Although raw flesh was not approved by the patriarch, Charles made an exception for the night.

Dante rubbed the bloodied organ on Austin's sealed lips – teasing him, *tormenting him.* Austin wriggled on the chair. He pushed up against the restraints with all of his might, exerting all of his energy to escape. His strength surged with the sound of a bone cracking – escape and vengeance were possible.

As he tortured their special guest with the meat, Dante said, "Oh, come on, sweetie, open up. Clyde enjoys his meat raw, maybe you will, too. Please, open up for mama. You don't want to make mama angry, do you? No, you wouldn't like that... You'll end up like this whore if you make me angry."

Austin's breathing intensified as he scowled at the eccentric man. Dante, the savage hitchhiker, was the source of the pain. If Austin had never picked him up, the couple would have been in Las Vegas – drinking, eating, gambling, *living.* Although the entire family was in his crosshairs, Dante was the prime target.

Austin glowered as the armrest and rope snapped off the chair. With the sharp end of the splintered armrest, Austin stabbed the bone into Dante's throat. The bone penetrated Dante's jugular with ease. Blood jetted from the wound, like crude oil erupting from a blowout. Wide-eyed, Dante plummeted to the ground.

Charles yelled, "Cheryl! Goddammit!"

Charles rushed to Dante's side. He examined the bone protruding from his neck and tried to stop the bleeding. Clyde teetered left-and-right, mystified by the attack. The pair had emerged from countless encounters unscathed, he did not know how to handle a fatal blow. As the family gathered around Dante, the photographer untied the restraints on the chair – one-by-one.

As he unwrapped the final rope, Austin took one final glance at Anna. He leaned forward and planted a kiss on her forehead – a final goodbye. Filled with reluctance, Austin quietly walked towards the other end of the table, then he glanced back. Oblivious,

Charles and Clyde argued indistinctly near Dante – a one-sided argument, of course. With one swift lunge, Austin escaped from the room.

Chapter Fourteen

The Great Escape

Austin stood towards the center of a hallway with his feet firmly planted on the dusty floorboards. He glanced around his newfound environment, trying to form an escape plan on the spot. He was not quick on his feet, his mind was not agile. Each plan led to a dead-end and a second wasted. *The butchers would be hunting soon,* he thought. The simple thought gave him enough reason to run – run, run, *run.*

Austin inhaled deeply, then he rushed down the hall. The sprint felt endless, like if he were hurtling through a nightmare. The walls were smeared with bloody handprints and scuffed by fingernail scrapings. Skin was plastered on the walls at regular intervals, treated like elegant paintings – Charles had the eye of a modern artist.

Austin shouted, "Shit!"

Recklessly lurching forward, he took a tumble only a few doors away from the dining room. He crawled ahead as he glanced back. He tipped over a makeshift console table. Instead of tipping over his own feet, he tumbled due to a set of human leg and foot bones. The appalling sight only made him crawl faster.

As he staggered to his feet, he pondered Anna's ultimate fate if the butchers survived the night. She was set to be reduced to a chair or a console table, or perhaps a foot rest. He could imagine Charles lounging on Anna's pile of bones after a long day's work. The image was despicable – *unacceptable.*

Austin muttered, "I can't let that happen... No, I can't let them do that. They have to die. They all have to die..."

Austin ran down the hall, wiping the sweat glistening on his brow. The hallway became longer with each step. He had lost count of the doors he passed. He felt like he was sprinting through a madhouse or running through a surreal realm – the world felt illusory. His mind was muddled by the atrocious night and his horrible memories.

Austin glanced back and whispered, "I'm fucking losing it..."

From afar, he could see he was only three doors away from the dining room – no more than 30 meters from the savage family. He shook his head and continued his brisk jog. His eyes widened as he spotted an opportunity. The door to his left was left slightly open. Austin slipped into the room, then he quietly shut the door behind him.

He planted his forehead on the door and whispered, "What do I do? How do I kill them? Anna, please, tell me what to do. Give me a sign. Show me the way..."

Austin's self-talk was interrupted by a ghastly gasp emerging from behind him. He loudly swallowed as he stepped away from the door. With narrowed eyes, he glanced back. There was a queen-sized bed with silk crimson sheets to the left towards the center of the room. A young woman, not much younger than Anna, laid atop the bed. The woman took his breath away. Sheer beauty could not accomplish such a feat. Even Anna failed to vacuum his lungs at first sight. The woman's physical condition rendered him momentarily speechless.

Austin rubbed his eyes as he walked towards the bed. He whispered, "What did they do to you?"

The brunette woman's legs were removed at the knees and her arms were dismembered at the elbows – a quadruple amputee. Her eyelids were crudely stitched shut. With each gasp of air, Austin could see her teeth were violently removed. Her tongue was also partially severed, cut in half with one foul snip. Her stomach was round and firm. The young woman was pregnant. She was brutalized and held hostage, used to continue the bloodline and create food.

Austin leaned over the bed and said, "I need you to..." He stepped back and shook his head, baffled. He said, "I don't know what I need you to do, really. I'm sorry. I don't... I don't know what to do. I've never been in this situation before. I want to take you with me. You understand? Tell me how to get out of here. Please, tell me something."

The woman did not respond. She gasped and trembled on the bed, then she settled on the mattress. Left and right, she slowly moved her head. Her moan of agony was faint and slow. She seemed to have the ability to talk, at least a bit more than Clyde, but she did not respond to Austin's pleas. Austin leaned closer as he stared at the woman's ear.

Through the darkness, he could see her ear was

blocked with a foreign body. He bit his bottom lip as he gently poked the object. She shuddered upon feeling the finger, but she did not respond. She was unaware of Austin's presence and intent. For all she knew, Charles was playfully prodding her – tormenting the woman.

In a dubious tone, Austin whispered, "Cement? They... They clogged your ears with cement?"

Austin was shocked – appalled and bewildered by the discovery. He was awed by the level of savagery the group reached. They continued to ascend beyond his wildest imagination. Aside from her olfactory perception and taste, the woman's senses were wiped. She could not see and she could not hear. Walking was also out of the question. Her nightmare was never-ending – a fate worse than death.

Infuriated, Austin said, "I'm going to avenge you, Helen, Anna, and... *and everyone else.* I'm going to kill all of these sick bastards. I promise."

Austin gently caressed the woman's forehead. The woman winced from the soft touch, but she quickly found some comfort in Austin's presence. Although she could not hear or see, she could still feel the aura of a person. She could feel Austin's kindness. For the first time since her kidnapping, she felt safe.

***

Despondent, Austin glanced at the door with narrowed eyes. He walked towards the neighboring wall, then he planted his ear on the barrier. He could hear the ruckus in the hallway. The old man and his remaining son were bickering and bantering. Considering Clyde's lack of speech, Charles was surely dominating the conversation.

Austin whispered, "What are you planning? Huh? What are you thinking, you sick bastards?"

Austin hopped away from the wall as the sound of a rattling chainsaw emerged. The roaring tool echoed through the large house, reverberating through the corridors and growling through the rooms. The noise was normal for everyday use, like a logger cutting down trees and slicing through branches for wood. The day was not like yesterday, though, and Clyde was not a logger. He sought to cut through flesh and slice through bone.

Austin sighed in relief as the chainsaw dwindled with a barrage of rumbling steps. *It must be Clyde,* he thought, *and he must be leaving.* The crepitating sound lowered to a faint buzz. The distraught man had moved far away from the bedroom. The photographer seized the opportunity, glancing around the room for a weapon. He huffed, then he nervously chuckled.

While making his disturbing discovery, he didn't notice parts of the bed frame were made of human bones. The bedposts caught his eye. The bedposts were crafted with humerus bones. He clenched his jaw and tugged on the bone. The hostage was not bothered by the bed's shaking. As the bone snapped, Austin stumbled back. The splintered bone was dusty and sharp – honed like a scalpel.

Austin whispered, "All of you will die from the bones of your victims..."

The sound of slow and heavy footsteps disrupted his contemplation. As the footsteps approached, he glanced around the room for a sturdy object. Across from the foot of the bed, beside a dormant fireplace, there was a chair comprised of human bones. Although he hated the thought of desecrating the remains, he knew his options were limited. He lifted the chair from the floor, then he heaved the furniture through the window. The glass shattered into a dozen sharp shards, twinkling with the moonlight.

Austin swiftly crawled under the bed. The hinges grated as the door violently swung open. Each step was slow and calculated – the butcher was vigilant. As the man approached, Austin peeked towards the window. To his utter relief, Charles protruded his head through the broken opening. Austin wanted to weaken the herd before attacking the mammoth monster known as 'Clyde.'

Charles glanced every which way, examining every nook and cranny on the adjacent hill. He peered towards the desolate motel, but to no avail. The captive was nowhere in sight. He could see Clyde running down the hill near the foyer of the house with the chainsaw over his head – chasing shadows, presumably.

Charles shouted, "He's out there somewhere, boy! You find him and you kill him! You slaughter that son of a bitch like you slaughtered his whore!" Clyde looked every which way, like if he were confused – *where is daddy's voice coming from?* Charles muttered, "Damn, moron... It should have been you,

you... you stupid motherfucker."

Charles glanced around the room, searching the darkest corners for the slightest clue. To his utter dismay, he found nothing. He could only assume the young photographer escaped his clutches through the broken window. He smirked upon spotting the brutalized woman. Fortunately for him, Austin did not touch her.

As he stared at the woman, Charles said, "You would have liked if he touched you, wouldn't you? That's what you wanted, right? Another man?" He turned towards the window and stared at the moon. He muttered, "You damn whore... I'll teach you a lesson."

Austin crawled out from under the bed, slithering like a snake in the grass. He stared at Charles' left ankle – his target. Beads of sweat dribbled down his brow, his breathing became restricted. He had a golden opportunity, one chance to immobilize the head of the household. He gritted his teeth, then he struck.

As Austin grabbed his leg, Charles glanced down and said, "What the hell are–"

Before he could finish, Austin sliced into Charles' Achilles tendon with the honed bone. The bone cut through his flesh like if he were slicing through paper. Blood gushed from the laceration as Austin sawed into Charles' heel. Even with blood splattering on his face, Austin couldn't stop himself. The bloodshed did not perturb him.

Charles shouted and stumbled forward. With such a careless action, he accidentally planted his palms on the broken window – stabbing himself with the sharp glass. The butcher spun in place, teetering every which way. Agony echoed from his sliced palms and mutilated ankle, crippling his entire body with a wave of pain.

As he reached the bottom of the hill, Clyde skidded to a stop and grunted. He turned towards the house as his father's bloodcurdling screech struck him. He moaned and glanced around the hill, baffled. He was ordered to find and kill a man, but his father was screaming for help. Although he only followed his father's direct commands, Clyde reluctantly hobbled towards the house. He already lost his sibling, who also happened to be his mother, and he refused to lose his father.

Charles staggered to his knees, grimacing and bellowing from the insufferable pain. Austin breathed heavily as he stepped behind the butcher. He grabbed a fistful of Charles' thin hair, then he pulled the man's head back. Charles cried, babbling indistinctly. He did not know the definition of mercy, but he had seen his victims beg. He simply replicated the moments before their unfortunate deaths, trying to convince the photographer to spare him.

Austin said, "You deserve to have a taste of your own medicine..."

Austin used the sharp bone to slice into Charles' scalp. Helen's image flashed in his mind, fueling his lust for vengeance. The sound of shredding skin was loud and unnerving. His hands were drenched in the spurting blood, like if he had just finished finger painting with red paint. Nothing could stop his rage, his conscience was killed with his girlfriend.

As he ripped Charles' scalp from his dome, Austin shouted, "You deserve to taste your own flesh!"

As the butcher bellowed, Austin shoved the bloodied scalp into Charles' mouth. He pushed and pulled on Charles' jaw, forcing him to chew the hair and flesh. Blood streamed down his chin and plopped on the floor as the man sobbed and coughed. Austin watched as Charles choked on his own scalp, gagging like a cat with a hairball.

Austin shouted, "Eat it! Eat it, you sick motherfucker!"

Clyde ran down the hall with his handy chainsaw, lurching towards Charles' cries. He stopped at the doorway to the bedroom and stared at his dying father with wide eyes – astonished. His father was supposed to be untouchable, his father was a god among men. He stomped and cried, weeping louder than the roaring chainsaw.

As Clyde ran into the room, Austin lifted Charles to his feet. He used the ravaged man as a human shield. In a fit of rage, Clyde blindly swung the chainsaw with all of his might. The chainsaw cut through Charles' shoulder, eating into his chest with each inch. Charles' eyes rolled to the back of his head as his body convulsed. He was dead within seconds. The chainsaw jammed, choking on the flesh.

Realizing he slaughtered his father, Clyde yammered, "N–N–N–N–N–N…"

Clyde could not finish the word. He couldn't utter

the only word in his vocabulary. The mixture of emotional pain and disability kept him from speaking. He could only stare into his father's bloodshot eyes as he tried to apologize for his mistake.

For a second, Austin felt bad for the young man. The pity, however, was short-lived. Austin grabbed the honed bone, then he lunged forward. He stabbed Clyde in the stomach. He pulled the bone out, then he stabbed him again – penetrating deeper than the first thrust. With one final thrust, the photographer stabbed the bone into Clyde's abdomen.

Austin slowly twisted the bone, maximizing the pain until the bone snapped. Clyde groaned as he wrestled with Austin, tightly holding the young photographer's wrists with his humongous hands. He cocked his head back like a walking pigeon, then he headbutted him. The force of the strike was enough to give both men a severe case of whiplash.

Austin staggered to his knees, dazed by the blow. Clyde glanced down at his stomach. He picked at the lingering pieces of bone trapped in his flesh. The fragments aggravated the wound, like shrapnel from a bomb. As Clyde struggled to tend to his grisly lacerations, Austin crawled out of the bedroom, escaping the carnage.

***

Austin walked down the hall, rubbing his forehead with his fingertips. The headbutt knocked him out of one nightmare and tossed him into another. *His head must be made of stone,* he thought. He bounced from wall-to-wall, struggling to regain his balance. He did not have the time to search for another advantage or explore the house. He could only work with the knowledge at hand.

Austin whispered, "The dining room... The dining room... *The kitchen...*"

Austin stumbled into the dining room, slamming the door behind him. He planted his back on the door and glanced around the room. He never wanted to return to the sinister area, but he had no other options. He walked alongside the long dining table, catching his breath and examining the shocking mayhem.

Helen swung from the ceiling, dead and scalped. He thought about cutting her down, but the action seemed useless. The woman, like the other victims, was already brutalized. Destroying the restraints would do nothing for a ravaged corpse. He closed his eyes and nodded at the woman – a motion of regret.

Austin clenched his jaw as he approached the other end of the table. Anna was slumped forward in her seat and Dante laid in a puddle of blood nearby. The pair were clearly dead, any attempts at resuscitation were futile. Dante's violent death did not matter – it was warranted after such a horrifying day. The mere sight of Anna, however, brought Austin to tears. He said his goodbyes, but he couldn't let her go.

As he walked past Anna, Austin whispered, "I'm sorry, sweetheart..."

Austin sniffled as he entered the kitchen through the door behind Anna. The kitchen was fairly simple – white tile flooring, white walls, and an island towards the center. There was a door on the parallel wall and another door to the left.

Austin staggered towards the island. He stood on his tiptoes and peered towards the door to the left. From the grimy brick walls and creaky staircase, he could see the door led to the basement. He glanced at the counters behind him. There was a large stainless steel stockpot on a stove. The flame was still hissing beneath the pot.

Austin whispered, "A weapon... I need a weapon."

The photographer nodded as he opened the door on the other side. Through the darkness, he could see a sofa, a coffee table, and a tube television. Except for the television, all of the furniture was made of human remains. *A living room,* he thought. He glanced back at the kitchen, peering towards the stove – an idea materialized.

Clyde grunted and moaned as he opened the dining room door with a mighty kick. He drew a machete with a long blade from a leather sheath at the back of his waistband. The machete had a 22-inch blade and the sheath was made of tanned human skin. The savage family did not waste any of their human resources.

The wicked man hobbled towards the kitchen door. He did not care for Helen or Anna – they were furniture and food, respectively. Upon spotting Dante's corpse, though, Clyde couldn't help but cry. He was flustered by the gory sight and angered by his failure. He shoved the kitchen door open and stopped at the doorway.

Clyde sniffled as he took one step forward. The

kitchen was surprisingly empty. As far as he was concerned, everything seemed to be in order. He walked towards the basement door with the machete over his head. He was prepared to strike anyone or anything in his path. To his utter disappointment, the basement seemed normal. He lowered the machete and whimpered.

With his shoulders and heels high, Austin quietly tiptoed into the kitchen from the living room. He could see Clyde rubbing his face and crying near the basement door, standing with his back to the captive. His sorrow was genuine, but it didn't matter. Austin bit his bottom lip and nodded as the opportunity presented itself.

Despondently staring down the staircase, Clyde muttered, "N–N–N–No..."

Austin shouted, "Yes, bastard, yes!"

Clyde turned back and moaned. Before he could lift the machete and swing, Austin poured the scorching stew from the stockpot on Clyde's body. Clyde screeched as the hot liquid burned his flesh. He staggered in reverse, then he took a tumble down the stairs. Each step cracked and howled from the man's weight.

Clyde continued to moan and weep, sprawled across the bottom of the stairs. Austin grabbed a chef knife from the counter. He had to finished the job, he had to wipe out the bloodline. He carefully descended into the basement, lunging over the shattered steps. He stopped at the final stair and stared down at Clyde.

Austin said, "Look at yourself." He furrowed his

brow, confounded. With a pinch of reluctance in his voice, he repeated, "Look at yourself..."

Clyde shriveled into the fetal position. With his hands wrapped around his head, he mewled like a newborn baby. The melancholic cries echoed through the dreary dungeon. The agony was sincere. The childish man did not understand deceit – he could not wear multiple faces like his brother. Austin examined Clyde with narrowed eyes. He had seen him before and he despised him for good reason.

Yet, his conscience finally awoke from a temporary slumber. He felt bad for the man. He could see Clyde was severely ill – abused, physically and mentally. He had emotional scars on his psyche. Forgiveness was not easy, though. The old man's final demands echoed through Austin's head: *you slaughter that son of a bitch like you slaughtered his whore!*

Austin sternly said, "I'll slaughter you like you slaughtered her."

Clyde cried as Austin tugged on his shoulder, forcing the butcher on his back. Austin pulled his arm back, then he stabbed down at Clyde's stomach. The honed knife penetrated deep into his gut with the powerful thrust. Austin clenched his jaw as he dragged the knife across the tender flesh, slicing a horizontal line across his abdomen – a reflection of Anna's fatal wound. Clyde wheezed and trembled on the ground, shocked by the attack.

Austin's arm trembled as he held his fingers over Clyde's wound. He wanted to stretch the wound and torture the vicious killer, but he was conflicted. As much as his mind called for vengeance, his heart could not respond with such savagery. Tears trickled from his eyes and plopped on Clyde's stomach.

As he tossed the knife aside, Austin said, "You... You deserve to die... Whatever they did to you, I'm sorry. It wasn't my fault, but you killed Anna. *You did that.* You killed the love of my life."

Austin wiped the tears from his eyes. He swallowed the lump in his throat, then he walked up the stairs. Surrounded by his victims, Clyde was left for dead in the grim dungeon.

Chapter Fifteen

Going Home

Austin returned to the main hall. He glanced towards his left as he contemplated his next move. He thought about the young woman in the bedroom. Despite the torture, she was still alive. Although the fact irked him, he knew he couldn't carry her out of the building in his condition. The police were her best option for survival. He figured Anna would have to wait for the police, too.

Austin whispered, "I'm sorry."

The young photographer walked down the hall to his right. He stared at the forest-green door at the end of the hallway. The door swung in the door frame, moving an inch with each gentle breeze. Early morning sunshine poured through the opening. His escape was not far, but he kept a vigilant mindset. *The killer always comes back to life,* he thought.

As he reached the final door in the hall before the exit, Austin stopped in his tracks. The sound of a feminine whimper seeped into the hallway from the neighboring room. His exit was only a few meters away, but curiosity got the best of him. He turned, then he gently shoved the door open.

From the doorway, Austin said, "It's you..."

Austin nervously smiled, fighting the urge to weep. Sitting in the corner of the bedroom, a young girl, no older than 11 years old, sat on the floor with her face to her knees. He recognized the black-haired girl from the photograph in the station wagon. The young girl was petrified, but she survived the massacre. She outlasted the butchers.

With a quivering lip and teary eyes, the girl asked, "Are... Are you one of them?"

Austin walked into the room with his hands up – a gesture of peace. The young girl squirmed closer to the wall, frightened. Austin nervously chuckled as he glanced at his hands. He was drenched in blood – face, hands, and clothing. He looked like a butcher.

Austin shook his head and said, "I'm not one of them, sweetie. I'm... I'm one of the good guys."

On the verge of breaking down, the girl asked, "Can... Can you take me to my mom and dad? *Please?*"

Austin sat on the bed and leaned forward with his elbows on his knees. He gazed into the girl's glowing brown eyes and said, "I can take you away from all of this. I know I don't look like a good guy right now, but I had to do some bad stuff to the bad guys. I know you've seen them before." The little girl sniffled and nodded. Austin asked, "What's your name, sweetheart?"

"Sam–Samantha..."

"Well, Samantha, my name is Austin. It's nice to meet you. If you trust me enough, you can follow me to the diner next door. I'm going to call the cops. They'll help us and anyone else in here. You understand? Do you want to get help with me?"

Samantha stared down at her blue sundress, pondering the question. She was visibly haunted by the experience. She had seen her fair share of bloodshed, especially from strangers. Yet, she trusted Austin. She was drawn to his kind aura. Through the blood, she could see the man was gentle and honest. He wasn't one of them.

Samantha nodded and said, "Okay."

Austin smiled and responded, "That's great, sweetheart. That's great..."

Austin and Samantha walked down the hallway, strolling towards the exit. The pair were exhausted from the trek. Samantha stared down at the groaning floorboards as she walked, watching her bare feet with caution. Austin placed his hands on his hips as he strolled onto the porch. He could see the motel and the diner down the hill – the finish line.

As Austin walked down the porch steps, Samantha said, "Austin..."

Austin turned towards Samantha and asked, "What is it, sweetie?"

Samantha twisted her foot and twiddled her thumbs. She asked, "Can you please hold my hand? *Please?*"

Austin smiled and nodded. He chuckled as he vigorously rubbed his palms on his shirt, trying his best to wipe off the clinging blood. Eyes filled with tears, he grabbed Samantha's small hand. The pair walked down the porch, then they strolled down the dirt pathway. As the sun began rising on the horizon, wailing police sirens echoed through the desert.

Austin stared at the rising sun and whispered, "Let's go home..."

Join the Mailing List

Congratulations! You made it out of Butcher Road! Through the blood and guts, you persevered. You're a survivor. But, are you sure the butchers are dead? There's only one way to find out. You can sign-up for my mailing list and receive all of my latest updates. You'll be the *first* to know about new novels, deep discounts, and free books! You'll only receive 1-2 emails a month, too. (Butchers don't like spam, I know.) It's greatly appreciated and requires little effort. Click here to sign-up: http://eepurl.com/bNl1CP

Dear Reader,

First and foremost, thank you for reading! I'm glad you finished the book. If you didn't finish it and you skipped to the end, I apologize for failing to meet your expectations. Regardless, your readership is truly invaluable to me. I can't thank you enough for picking *Butcher Road* over the millions of books available to you. This was a product of genuine passion and it's gratifying to know someone has read the book from beginning to end. *Butcher Road*, like the rest of my work, was fueled by my love for storytelling and dark fiction. I pride myself in delivering uncompromising horror stories. However, I never intend on offending or appalling anyone. If you were offended by the content in this book, please accept my sincerest apologies.

Butcher Road was inspired by slasher horror films. Particularly, this book was inspired by *The Texas Chainsaw Massacre* and *Psycho*. If you love horror films, you probably noticed the elements I wanted to recreate from those movies, such as the hitchhiker and motel concepts. Of course, some would argue these aren't exactly your traditional slasher movies. Most people associate slasher with *Halloween* or *Friday the 13th.* Although I love those series (for completely different reasons), I felt like focusing on a drearier style of slasher. I wanted to create something grim.

There were a few tropes I obviously tried my best

to ignore – maybe I failed, maybe I succeeded. The first cliché was the cast of characters. I was never a fan of the obnoxious characters that often plague modern slashers. In other words, I'm not a big fan of douchebags – is there a more appropriate word for those people? I don't know. Anyway, the only characters I wanted you to hate in this story were the butchers. Although our protagonists made a few questionable choices, I didn't want you to hate them. In a lot of slashers, you kind of end up rooting for a high body count – especially because some characters may irk you. I wanted to focus more on suspense and I wanted the few deaths in this story to unnerve.

I also ignored the whole 'gratuitous sex' trope in this book. I know, I know, it's part of the modern slasher DNA. In this case, however, I felt it would add *nothing* to the story. Secondly, I'm not great at writing erotic scenes, so I thought it would turn out ill-fitted. It was best to ignore it and focus solely on the horror. I did, however, allude to some abuse in the book – especially the abuse of the young unnamed girl in the bedroom. Abuse is never a pretty subject, but I felt it added to the human horror more than a sex scene. Again, maybe I failed, maybe I succeeded.

Anyway, if you enjoyed this book, *please* leave an honest review on Amazon.com. Your review is incredibly significant. In fact, my career *depends* on your review. Your review will help me improve on future books and it will help other readers find this book. The more readers I garner, the more I can write. So, if you like this book, a review will help me release more. It will also allow me to gauge interest for certain genres and themes. Would you like to read more slasher-horror books? Was this book too violent? Do you prefer a slow-burn buildup to a grisly climax or do you want the deaths scattered throughout the book? Do you prefer sex scenes in your slashers? Answering these types of questions in your review will help me improve. Even simply letting me know you liked the book helps me improve – it's a morale boost. Your words have the power to influence my writing – please use them wisely.

Also, feel free to share this book with your friends and family. Tweet it to your followers on Twitter, share it with your friends and family on Facebook, lend it to them, or even read it to them over the phone or video chat. Birthday, holiday, or special event coming up? Buy them a copy as a gift. Word-of-mouth is a superb method in supporting independent authors – and it's mostly *free*. My lifestyle consists of cheap noodles, tap water, and my neighbor's TV. (I need binoculars, I can't get caught peeping through their window again.) I need your support to sustain this 'thrifty' lifestyle.

Finally, if you enjoy scary stories, feel free to visit my Amazon's author page. I've published over a *dozen* horror anthologies. Looking for a violent revenge/vigilante justice thriller? I highly recommend reading my shocking thriller, *Mr. Snuff.* Enjoy serial killer fiction? You should check out my horror/thriller, *Sinister Syndromes.* The book follows two killers on opposite ends of the spectrum. When they clash, blood is spilled throughout a dilapidated city. Furthermore, many of my books are available on Kindle Unlimited! I publish books frequently, so please keep your eyes peeled for the next release. I have a slate of books ready to release in 2016, including more serial killer novels – some more disturbing than others. Once again, thank you for reading. Your readership has kept me going through my darkest times and I am forever grateful.

Until our next venture into the dark and disturbing,
Jon Athan

P.S. If you have questions (or insults), you'll receive the quickest and most efficient response via Twitter @Jonny_Athan. If you're an aspiring author, I'm always happy to lend a helping hand. I know how difficult it can be to get started, so feel free to ask. You can also *like* my Facebook page and talk to me there. Thanks again!

Made in United States
Orlando, FL
05 March 2023

30676928R00104